FULLY VETTED

FARM FRESH COZY MYSTERIES, BOOK 7

SUMMER PRESCOTT

SUMMER PRESCOTT BOOKS PUBLISHING

Copyright 2024 Summer Prescott Books

All Rights Reserved. No part of this publication nor any of the information herein may be quoted from, nor reproduced, in any form, including but not limited to: printing, scanning, photocopying, or any other printed, digital, or audio formats, without prior express written consent of the copyright holder.

**This book is a work of fiction. Any similarities to persons, living or dead, places of business, or situations past or present, is completely unintentional.

CHAPTER ONE

"I can't believe the twins came to visit, finally." Entrepreneurial market farmer, Shea Beaumont, beamed at her bestie from across the table at their formerly favorite bistro. "It was beyond amazing to have them with me again."

"It only took them two years to make the trip," Trish, teased.

"I know, but I told myself that they're broke and busy college students," Shea replied. "But I also think that their dad showing up here and landing in federal prison might have a little bit to do with it."

"Makes sense, and now you have a semi-permanent house guest," Trish said with a wicked grin. She pushed the overcooked crust of her spinach quiche across her plate.

"I know! Carrie was so difficult when she first got here that I wondered if we'd ever have a good relationship again and now, she's staying on to help me with the farm while she gets her career started. I can hardly believe it." Shea shook her head, her eyes sparkling.

She took a small bite of her spinach casserole, made a face, then leaned in a bit before speaking. "I don't think this place will ever be the same without Dylan," she whispered sadly.

"I know. This is the worst quiche I have ever had here," Trish replied sighing.

She instinctively looked for Dylan Branch, the outspoken owner of Farm to Fork, the farm-to-table restaurant in the small town of Pawnee, but he'd been the victim of a murderous distributor a few months back. The restaurant, and the town just didn't seem the same without him.

"If Dylan had ever heard you say something like that, he would have booted both of us out and would never have bought so much as another stalk of celery from either of us again," Shea said, her heart aching as she smiled sadly, remembering the crusty character who had become a friend.

"That's the truth." Trish laughed softly. "Maybe we'll need to be the town terrors now."

"I think we have a good start at that." Shea chuckled.

"Where are you headed after breakfast?" Trish asked.

"The Feed and Seed and then the vet clinic. Dr. Bev asked me to stop by her office to pick up some meds because one of the nanny goats has an infection."

"I'll walk to the Feed and Seed with you," Trish offered. "I have to pick up some things for Barry, and maybe I can walk off a few of the calories that all of the excess lard in that quiche crust gave me."

The two of them took turns treating each other to meals, so this time Shea paid for their less than satisfactory breakfast and followed Trish out into the warmth of the Oklahoma spring day. It had warmed up since their arrival at the bistro, enough so that Shea slipped out of her hoodie and tied it around her waist, enjoying the feel of the sun on her bare arms. After they crossed the road and entered the farm store, Shea left Trish in the bulk seed section while she ducked into the garden department.

Thanks to her early planning and planting, the bins at her farm stand were already filled with beets, baby carrots, peas, and scallions. The demand for her microgreens had nearly doubled since she began selling them and she already needed to replace the planting trays that she used for the tender greens that grew in the large greenhouse next to the barn. She filled a shopping cart with as many trays as she could find and headed back to the seed aisle.

"Wow, girl, you aren't messing around. Did you buy them out?" Trish asked, her drawl thick.

"Yeah, actually, I did." Shea grinned.

"I told you this would happen." Trish smiled, crossed her arms, and nodded sagely.

"You told me what would happen?" Shea peered over the stack of trays in her cart.

"I told you when you first started working in your farm stand that you'd wind up thinking like a farmer, and now look at you. You've expanded your little operation into a real business," Trish said proudly. "And you're thinking like a local."

Shea shook her head and laughed. "I think that depends on who you ask. I'm pretty sure there are plenty of people around here who still think I'm too much of a city girl to make a farm work. They're probably taking bets on how soon I'll fail."

"Well, if you hear of anybody who is, let me know. I could win a fortune on that gamble." Trish chuckled. "But I've gotta get going. Y'all ready to head out?"

"I don't think I could put anything else in my cart if I tried, so yeah, I guess so," Shea replied, following her toward the checkout lanes.

They paid for their purchases and headed outside, with Shea staggering a bit beneath the weight of the trays.

"I guess I didn't really think this through when I suggested a walk to the Feed and Seed," she muttered, peering around the heavy stack that she carried.

"Amen, sister. That's the last time I listen to your suggestion," Trish agreed, hauling heavy bags of seed to her SUV.

The two made it to their vehicles, perhaps a bit more sweaty than they'd been when they started out, but otherwise unharmed. Shea set the trays in the back of her Jeep and waved at Trish as she headed out of the parking lot, then made her way over to the vet clinic a few blocks away.

Corky Sims, the receptionist at the clinic, took her job very seriously and when Shea came in, she practically dashed toward the reception desk from the supply room behind it. Her blond ringlets bounced as she moved, and she beamed like a contestant in a Miss America pageant.

"What can I do for you today, Ms. Beaumont?" she asked.

"Good morning, Corky," Shea replied, trying to hide her amusement at the receptionist's enthusiasm. "I just need to pick up a prescription for one of my goats."

"You got it, ma'am. Just hang on for one sec, and I'll be right back," was the cheerful reply. Corky disappeared down the hall toward the office just as another vet tech, Chelsea, emerged from the clinic side tugging on a heavy black leash.

At the other end of the leash was the largest dog Shea had ever seen. Its freshly groomed fur was fluffed up on end, giving it the appearance of a giant, cuddly teddy bear. The dog panted loudly and sat down, seeming to smile at Shea as she stood by the front desk.

She bit back a chuckle as she watched the vet tech tug harder on the leash in a seemingly vain attempt to get the furry beast to move.

"Come on, Tiny," Shea heard Chelsea grumble. "Your mama is waiting for you in the car. Can you please just cooperate with me for once?"

Shea couldn't help herself; she chuckled when the dog yawned and flopped over on his side, clearly begging for a belly rub. He wagged his tail, thumping it soundly against a cardboard display of flea and tick powder that teetered precariously over him and Chelsea.

"I think she has a treat for you, you big lunk," Chelsea said in a frustrated, sing-song voice, tugging hard on the leash, putting all of her weight into it. Shea hoped that the leash didn't snap under the strain, but the grumpy tech managed to get the dog onto his feet. She took the leash in both hands and put it over her shoulder, leaning forward and grunting with effort until she'd gone roughly three feet closer to the outside door.

"Would you like some help?" Shea asked, biting back a giggle.

"No, I'd prefer that you stand there gawking," Chelsea snapped, her eyes narrowed. "That's what really helps me out in this situation."

"I was going to offer to open the door for you," Shea replied, eyebrows raised.

"Well, how special." Chelsea rolled her eyes and sighed loudly. "Could you please open the door? If it isn't too much to ask of you, that is."

Shea clamped her mouth shut for a moment, resisting the urge to employ a verbal flame-thrower as she headed toward the door.

"Of course. If it'll help Tiny out, I'd be glad to help," she finally replied, raising an eyebrow and glancing over her shoulder to give the tech a meaningful look.

As soon as the door was opened the dog let out an eardrum shaking woof and sprinted for the parking lot, dragging Chelsea after him with the end of the leash still wrapped around her wrist, her auburn ponytail flying out behind her.

Shea didn't feel a bit guilty for somewhat enjoying the dog's shenanigans and hoped that it might teach the surly tech to be just a bit more kind to both humans and animals. She returned to the reception desk to wait for Corky.

"Shea, I'm afraid there was a mistake in the order for today," Dr. Bev said, coming around the corner with a file folder a few seconds later. "I honestly don't know what's going on with my inventory these days, but Corky couldn't find the ointment that I ordered for you."

"Oh, okay… should I drop by again tomorrow, then? It'll have to be later on in the day," Shea said, thinking aloud. "Saturdays are the busiest days at the farmer's market by far, so I'd have to wait until afterward."

"Oh dear, I'm afraid that won't work. We close at noon, but I definitely want you to start using this on your nanny goat as soon as possible" Dr. Bev replied, frowning.

She tapped her pen of the file folder, then smiled when Chelsea reentered the clinic. "Okay, I know how we can handle this," the vet said, seeming relieved. "I'll just have Chelsea deliver the ointment to you at the farmer's market on her way home. You drive past there anyway, don't you, Chels?"

Chelsea took a breath and ground her teeth for a couple of seconds before replying. Some of her hair had come loose from her ponytail and she had a less than positive expression. "Sure thing," she said finally, her plastic smile looking as though it pained her. "I can think of nothing I'd rather do after work tomorrow than deliver a prescription to this nice lady."

CHAPTER TWO

"Good morning," Shea greeted Helen Porter, one of the other market vendors, with a wave when she pulled up at the end of Shea's driveway just after six in the morning. Trish was unloading her own truck and stocking her stand, which was of course right next to Shea's, when the older woman arrived.

Helen's farm stand was across the two-lane rural highway, so Shea brewed a fresh cup of coffee for her and jogged over with it. Ever since the untimely death of her wayward husband, Helen's attitude toward the general public had shifted a bit. Even if she couldn't quite be what most folks would consider overtly kind, she was far less crusty than she had been…on most days. Shea and Trish had made it their mission to do something nice for her on occasion, mostly just to be nice, but also to see what her reaction might be on any given day.

"What's this for?" Helen asked, staring at the steaming mug as though it might bite her when Shea set it on the front counter of her farm stand.

"Just something to warm you up," Shea replied kindly. "It's a bit chilly this morning."

"Oh. Well then…thank you," Helen said. Shea could swear she saw one corner of her mouth twitch upward for a brief moment.

"I count it as a smile," Shea whispered to Trish when she returned to her stand across the road.

"It was hard to tell from this far away, but I think you can count that as a win," Trish replied with a chuckle, sipping the coffee that she'd poured for herself.

Shea had just started filling green plastic pint-sized vegetable baskets with the leftover vegetables from the day before when Carrie, the twin who had decided to work on the farm with her mother, appeared.

"Morning, sunshine," she greeted her daughter, who still looked like she'd just rolled out of bed.

"Ugh," Carrie grunted, sitting down on one of the barstools behind the counter and staring at the coffee pot.

"It won't pour itself," Shea teased, weighing baskets of baby carrots and arranging them on the shelf in front of the front counter.

Carrie blinked and went over to the coffee pot, found the biggest mug under the rough hewn cabinet that it rested upon, and filled it, leaving just enough room for fresh cream.

"That rooster is going to be the death of me," she muttered, setting down her coffee after a large gulp and grabbing handfuls of goat's milk soaps to stack on the counter. When she was done with the soaps, she arranged the goat's milk candles on the opposite corner, sipping her coffee while she sorted the jars by scent.

"Oh? I thought you two were best buddies," Shea said, grinning. "What did he do now?"

"The same thing he always does. He woke me up by making that horrendous racket beneath my window. But, I'll show you. It's only a matter of time and I'm going to have him trained like a show dog," Carrie promised, hiding a smile.

She started arranging the pickles and preserves next, while Shea continued to set out fresh vegetables.

Shea laughed aloud. "Good luck with that. I swear, if you teach that ridiculous bird to do tricks, I'm going to take video and put it on my blog. We'll go viral."

"Yeah, especially since you've taken video of him launching sneak attacks on you," Carrie said, chuckling. "He's an animal. Animals always love me, so he'll come around, just wait and see."

"Oh, I'll be waiting for sure."

"Holy cow, look at the line of people pulling up," Carrie exclaimed, her mouth dropping open as she craned her neck to see further down the road. "There are cars as far as I can see, coming from both directions."

"Welcome to Saturday at the market," Shea said, taking a deep breath to gear up for the morning rush. "We'll be fine. Just restock anything that runs low."

"What if we run out of something?" Carrie asked, wide-eyed.

"Put something else out in its place," Shea said with a shrug. "Running out is the goal." She smiled.

"I should've had more coffee," Carrie said, shaking her head.

They sold out of the baby carrots and most of the other vegetables in the front bins within a couple of hours, working side by side as a team. It was the easiest and most efficient market day that Shea had experienced since she first opened the stand.

"I think we might be ready to close up shop before lunchtime," Shea mused when Trish came over during a lull.

"Don't you have that mean girl who works for Dr. Bev stopping by around noon?" Trish asked, leaning wearily against the door frame. Her baked goods had been flying off the shelves as shoppers hungry for breakfast snapped up the heavenly selections.

"Oh, right." Shea nodded. "I almost forgot."

"Mean girl?" Carrie asked, looking up from re-arranging the remaining jars of pickled beets.

"She's a vet tech who was apparently in a very bad mood when I saw her yesterday," Shea explained.

"She was straight up rude," Trish translated.

"I see. Well, just let me know if she needs a dose of humility from a bona fide city girl," Carrie said with a smirk.

Another wave of customers swarmed the stands, and by noon more than half of the pickles had sold, along with the rest of the vegetables in the bins and several soaps and candles. Shea was more than pleased with the day's sales but was slightly anxious that Chelsea from Dr. Bev's office hadn't stopped by yet with the medication for the nanny goat. It was bad enough that a mistake had been made, resulting in a delay, but Shea didn't want to leave the goat untreated for any longer than she had to.

The sun beat down without mercy on the roof of the farm stand as she and Carrie loaded up the flatbed trailer with the remaining supplies to take up to the barn refrigerator, and Shea definitely regretted her wardrobe choices, having dressed for the cool morning rather than the warm afternoon. She wanted nothing more than to head back to the house for a change of clothes and a quick cool shower before she and Carrie had a bite to eat, then tackled the afternoon chores.

A small crowd of shoppers lingered at the four other farm stands that were still open, browsing as though they had all the time in the world.

"Must be nice." Shea sighed, unaware that she'd spoken the thought aloud.

"Yeah, but think about it this way…you wouldn't know what to do with a bunch of spare time if you didn't have a farm to take care of," Carrie teased, nudging her mother playfully.

"Yep, I chose this and I love it. I just have to remind myself of that fun fact occasionally," Shea said wryly.

"And of course, without fail because you and I closed early, here comes another car," Trish said, inclining her head toward a small vehicle that was slowing down, but not much. "Coming in a little fast, though." She frowned.

The car stopped rather suddenly, kicking up a spray of gravel.

"No worries, it's just Chelsea from Dr. Bev's office," Shea replied, relieved that the goat meds had arrived before she'd made the trek back to the barn and house.

She turned to the fridge and pulled out a box that she'd filled with fresh veggies that she planned to give Chelsea for taking the time to deliver the ointment. She smiled as the tech approached.

"Hey - good afternoon," Shea said brightly, determined to let bygones be bygones. "Thanks for making the trip…" she began.

"Here," Chelsea interrupted, tossing a plastic bag across the counter at her. "Now you can treat your goat and put her right back to work for you."

"I'm sorry?" Shea said, startled by the response. "Is there a problem?"

Chelsea picked up a goat's milk candle with two fingers and held it up for a moment, grimacing.

"Is this why you're milking that poor goat until she's so chafed that she gets an infection? In my book that makes you a terrible human being." She slammed the candle back down on the counter and stared at Shea. Carrie whipped off the apron she'd been wearing and headed toward the counter, clearly ready for battle.

"Now you just wait a hot minute," Shea said, glaring at the young woman while holding Carrie back with one hand. "You know exactly nothing about how I treat my animals."

"Really? I actually think that I have a pretty good idea." Chelsea's voice dripped with accusation. She tapped on the counter next to the bag of ointment between them. "That's a powerful antibiotic gel. You had to have milked that poor goat well past a typical milking schedule for her to wind up with the kind of massive infection that this medicine is used to treat."

"Well, you may think you know everything, honey, but you'd be wrong. That goat isn't even used to produce milk for products. She happened to give birth to triplets three weeks ago and those babies are wearing her out," Shea said, eyebrows raised in warning. "Next time you think about accusing someone of mistreatment, you might want to ask your boss about their situation first. She's the one who prescribed the ointment as a precaution when the nanny started looking a little swollen."

"Yeah, right. I'm sure that's all it is." Chelsea rolled her eyes. "I'm sure you made all of this stuff from canned goat's milk that you bought at the grocery store."

Shea looked up. Almost as if they could just smell a hint of drama in the air, a small crowd had gathered close and stood taking it all in. If she wanted to maintain the reputation she'd built for herself in this town, Shea was going to have to just take a deep breath and let it go.

"You need to leave," she told the vet tech calmly. "I'm not abusing my animals, nor will I ever do so. Thanks for your concern. Before you go, I saved some veggies from today's crop for you. Let me just go get them from the fridge," Shea said, her smile feeling entirely at odds with the emotions that were currently roiling through her.

"You can stuff your veggies where the sun don't shine, lady. I don't want a thing from you, and you can bet that I'll get the word out to people about how you treat your animals," Chelsea hissed.

As Carrie, ready to give the young woman a piece of her mind, darted toward the door of the farmstand, Trish stepped directly into her path and stopped her in her tracks with a look and a hand on her arm.

"Look, why don't we all just take a short walk up the driveway and Chelsea can see the happy goats for herself," Trish suggested, giving both mother and daughter that special look of hers that said, 'please keep quiet and let me handle this.' "You're a vet tech after all, right?" She turned her steely gaze toward Chelsea.

Shea glared at her best friend, folded her arms, and shook her head. "After the way she's been acting toward me, there's no way in the world that I'd let her step foot on my land to see the goats or any other animals on this farm," she said, shooting a dagger of a glance toward Chelsea. "In fact, if Dr. Bev doesn't fire her for being absolutely horrific to a customer, I'm going to have to look for another vet."

"Awww…what a shame. We'll miss you," Chelsea smirked.

When Trish DeMarcus's Oklahoma accent grew profound, it was a clear signal that someone was in trouble, and when she spoke to Chelsea her accent was so thick you could have cut it with a knife and had it for supper with potatoes and a nice salad.

"Honey, you got about ten seconds to get your hind end outta here before I have to take my earrings off."

CHAPTER THREE

Shea woke before Clarence even sounded his daily alarm the next morning and was surprised to smell coffee. After dressing in work clothes that she didn't mind getting muddy, she headed down to the kitchen to find that Carrie was already up, dressed, and looking fairly coherent. More importantly, she'd made coffee and was having a cup before going out to help with the morning chores.

"To what do I owe the pleasure?" Shea asked, gratefully accepting a steaming mug of coffee and settling in at the kitchen table.

"This is my life now." Carrie shrugged, stifling a yawn. "If farm life means getting up early, then I'll be getting up early." She smiled ruefully.

"It took me a while to get used to it, too," Shea confided. "But it gets easier, I promise."

"Then I'll have something to look forward to." Carrie chuckled.

They both jumped when Clarence, who sounded like he was standing right below the kitchen window, let out a full-volume trumpet blast of a crow.

"Think we offended him by getting up so early?" Carrie asked, grinning.

"Nah, I think he enjoys startling the daylights out of us." Shea made a face.

"Well, I don't know about you, but that adrenalin was just what I needed to get me jump-started," Carrie commented, rising as she downed the last gulp of coffee. She put her cup in the sink and headed for the door. "Chore time," she said. "And poor lil ole Clarence is going to find out what life is like when the hens get fed before he does."

"Oh boy, this one ought to be interesting," Shea replied. "I'll be out shortly."

She stood at the window, drinking her coffee after Carrie left, keeping an eye on Clarence. The spindly old rooster could be pretty aggressive when he wanted to be, and Shea didn't know what she might do with him if he dared to hurt Carrie.

Samson, their sweet-natured Golden Retriever had been snoozing on the front porch, but as soon as he heard the kitchen door, he came trotting around to greet Carrie with sloppy kisses, paws on her shoulders as she giggled and stroked his ears. Clarence and Samson weren't exactly friends either.

Making sounds low in his throat, the rooster stalked toward them. Samson dropped back down onto all fours and stood beside Carrie, his head lowered.

"It's okay, big fella," Carrie told the dog, scratching the top of his head while staring Clarence down.

"Now you listen to me, buddy," she began, giving Clarence her most stern look. "We're not going to have any drama this morning. It's too early for me to deal with all of that, got it?"

Clarence continued his march toward them, his head bobbing up and down. Shea had seen that move before. The rooster meant business, which likely meant that either Carrie, Samson, or both of them were about to be on the receiving end of his sharp beak. Knowing that her daughter would be irritated if she went out to intervene, Shea stayed in her spot at the window, even after her coffee was gone.

Clarence was about three feet from them when he raised his wings, a sure sign that he was about to strike.

"No!" Carrie ordered sharply, pointing at him.

Clarence flapped his wings and let out an earthshattering siren of a squawk. Carrie didn't move. Her finger was still pointing. Samson barked.

"It's okay. Sit, buddy," she murmured to the dog. "I've got this, don't worry."

"Clarence, settle down," she directed, taking a step toward him. The old rooster stood his ground and squawked again. "I mean it, Clarence. You're going to be nice." Carrie's voice was still stern but was softer as she inched forward. Shea held her breath. If that cranky old bird dared to peck her daughter…

Clarence slowly raised his wings and Carrie firmly told him no. He lowered them again, looking a bit confused. His voice was much quieter when he hollered again.

"Now, we're going to go to the coop to feed the hens and you're going to be nice, got it?" Carrie said, moving even closer to the befuddled bird. Silence. He didn't crow. He didn't move.

"Good." Carrie nodded. "Okay, Samson, let's go feed the chickens," she said to the dog, who looked up at her, then looked at the rooster and cocked his head to the side. "Don't worry, I'm not going to let him get you," Carrie promised, striding forward and stepping around a still confused Clarence. Samson trotted next to her, glancing behind them repeatedly. When he let out a low woof, Carrie turned to see Clarence sprinting toward the dog. She stepped directly into his path and barked out his name.

"Clarence!"

The rooster stopped and stared at her.

"We're going to go into the coop, but I don't want you behind poor Samson. Go on ahead of us." She pointed. Clarence stared. "You heard me. Get on up there." She pointed again.

Shea's mouth dropped open in shock when Clarence gave Carrie a dirty look and proceeded to do exactly what he'd been told.

"You'd better watch that attitude, mister," Carrie warned, heading toward the coop with Clarence leading the way.

Shea put her coffee mug in the sink and headed outside, shaking her head in disbelief. "That's my girl," she murmured proudly.

"Hey, Rooster Whisperer," she greeted Carrie when she entered the chicken coop.

Clarence had settled into one of the nesting boxes and was seemingly intentionally refusing to even look at the humans and the dog who were currently invading his territory while he waited for his turn to be fed.

"You saw that, huh?" Carrie grinned, brushing off her hands after feeding the cantankerous bird.

"I'm still trying to believe it, but yes, I saw it. When did you get into voodoo?" Shea teased.

"No voodoo required," Carrie said, chuckling. "We just had to understand each other, that's all."

"Gee, why didn't I ever think of that?" Shea shook her head and followed her daughter out of the chicken coop.

"Yeah, why didn't you?" Carrie shot a mischievous glance over her shoulder and cracked up.

Samson joined in the merriment by letting out a happy woof, which made Clarence flap his wings in protest, but aside from that, the rooster didn't utter a peep.

"Don't make me chase you to the goat pen," Shea replied.

Carrie let the two of them into the goat pen and Shea was once again amazed. Even the most rambunctious young goats greeted her respectfully, gently even. There was no butting against her knees or rushing at her to make her stumble. She spoke to them in low tones that seemed to almost hypnotize them.

Shea stopped to watch, a lump forming in her throat.

After greeting each goat personally, Carrie glanced up and caught Shea's eye.

"What?" she asked, with an amused smile.

Shea cleared her throat before speaking. "It's just… you're really good at this. I mean, really, really good."

Carrie blushed, shrugged, and looked down at one of the baby goats who was bleating for her attention.

"Yeah, well, that's probably because I learned from the best. Have you checked the nanny goat yet? Her triplets look like they're doing well with nursing from the other nannies."

"Oh good, let's go take a look at her. Dr. Bev said that I'll need to very carefully express her milk and dispose of it because of the medication," Shea replied, back into chore mode.

Mother and daughter knelt beside the nanny in her separate enclosure and peered underneath her.

"Oh wow, it really looks like the medicine is helping," Carrie exclaimed, sounding relieved.

"Thank goodness," Shea agreed, nodding.

"Do you want me to go water the veggies in the greenhouse while you're milking?" Carrie asked, standing up and brushing straw from the knees of her lightweight cargo pants.

"You know what…why don't you leave that for later? I'd love it if you made more coffee instead. We can enjoy a cup on the porch for a bit before we finish up the chores. It's Sunday, so there's no rush today, since the market is closed."

"Oh man, I think you read my mind." Carrie grinned. "Fresh coffee, I'm on it. I'll meet you on the porch. Are there any cookies left from what Trish brought over yesterday?"

"I think so, check the pantry," Shea replied, grabbing a milking pail and getting to work.

With her coffee steaming in her cup, Shea gazed over the farm and settled back in her chair, taking a bite of one of Trish's amazing chocolate chip cookies. Carrie sat in the chair that Trish usually used, and they propped their feet up on a small stool in front of the wicker table that was between them.

Shea felt reflective and was content to just soak in the moment. Life was busy and full, and sometimes a little bit crazy, but by and large, she was the happiest she had ever been. The fields were filled with the color of life, and it positively made her heart soar to see her daughter caring for the animals and having them respond. The farm had grown, as had her many enterprises, and with Carrie's help, in addition to borrowing some of Trish's teenagers to use as paid farmhands, Shea was more than confident that not only could she handle it, but that she could cheerfully continue to expand. Life on the farm was definitely looking up. Shea was perfectly at peace…until she wasn't.

One thing was certain. It didn't matter that Shea considered Deputy Andrea Salt a good friend, and it also didn't matter that her relationship with Sheriff Seth Grayson was continuing to blossom in the sweetest of ways; when she saw the familiar sight of the white sheriff's department squad car slow down and pull into her driveway, with no advance notice, her heart went to her throat.

The moist and tender bite of cookie that she'd been enjoying turned to sawdust in her mouth. There might be nothing wrong. Seth might be bringing her lunch, or just stopping by to say hello. But Shea was human, and the sight of that car coming up the drive caused a visceral reaction that was pretty much the same as if she'd seen flashing lights in her rearview mirror.

"Are you expecting someone?" Carrie asked in a low voice.

Shea shook her head.

"I'm going to go in and take a quick shower," Carrie said tactfully, apparently having noticed Shea's reaction. "Do you want a refill on your coffee before I go?"

"No, go ahead, honey. If I need more coffee in a minute, I'll grab some, thanks," Shea replied, still watching the car's progress.

The front door closed softly behind Carrie as the car pulled to a stop, Shea was slightly shocked to see Seth step out of it, dressed in his uniform. He looked amazing, as always, but she'd become so accustomed to seeing him in regular clothes that it gave her the impression that the reason behind his visit might not be a good one.

"Good morning, Shea," he said, closing the car door and heading for the porch. He stopped at the bottom of the steps, his hand on the banister. His warm Oklahoma drawl made her insides shiver, but she didn't miss the fact that his usual admiring grin was absent.

"Morning," Shea replied, sitting up and dropping her feet down from their perch. "Want some coffee? Carrie just made a fresh pot a few minutes ago, and she's actually getting pretty good at it." She smiled nervously, realizing that she was babbling a bit. What was with her? It was just Seth, for crying out loud.

Yet, she couldn't quite shake the feeling that something was wrong.

"I'm afraid I can't," he said, his expression grave. "I'm here in an official capacity, unfortunately."

Her intuition confirmed, Shea swallowed hard. "You are?" she said, nervous little knots forming in her stomach. "Why? What's wrong? Did something happen?"

Seth sighed, dropping his gaze to the bottom step.

"I need you to tell me where you were last night, Shea," he replied, avoiding her questions.

"Where I was last night?" Shea's brows rose. "I was here, where I always am. Just another normal night with animals and chores. Why are you asking me that, Seth? That question doesn't get asked without a reason behind it, particularly in an official capacity," Shea said, folding her arms, brows raised.

Seth leaned against the banister, raising his eyes to meet hers. "I don't suppose there'd be anyone around here who could corroborate your whereabouts last night…"

"Corroborate?" Shea stared at him in disbelief, but he held her gaze, clearly waiting for an answer. "No, not unless you count talking on the phone with Trish," she replied finally, feeling hurt and desperately trying not to let it show. "After we chatted for a bit, I came inside, wrote a new blog post and then went to bed. That took maybe an hour. I mean, Carrie was here the whole time, if that matters."

"Considering the fact that she's your daughter, no, it doesn't really matter. Where were you, specifically, when you wrote the blog post?" Seth asked.

"I was in my office like I usually am. Seth, what on earth is going on? Why are you asking me so many questions about where I was last night?" Shea frowned.

"Because there have been reports that you had a pretty negative interaction with Chelsea Russell, the vet tech from Dr. Bev's office, yesterday," Seth replied, baffling her.

Shea frowned. "Well, yes, that happened at the end of the farmer's market, because she was insufferably rude," she said, remembering. "And plenty of customers witnessed it, so I'm not surprised that it got back to you through the grapevine, but I'm still failing to see what that has to do with where I might have been last night."

"Yeah, there were definitely plenty of witnesses. And more than one of them called the office to let me know about it after word got out that a body was discovered at the veterinary clinic early this morning," Seth replied, looking pained.

Shea felt vaguely faint, and her stomach churned. "A body? Oh my gosh. Is Dr. Bev…I mean, is she… okay?"

"Depends on how you mean that," Seth said grimly. "Dr. Bev is the one who discovered the body in the lab at the clinic. Chelsea Russell was the victim."

Utterly stunned, Shea's eyes went wide, and she slumped against the back of her chair, mouth open, shaking her head. "I can't believe it," she said slowly. "She was literally here just yesterday, and now she's dead? That's just…crazy."

Seth cleared his throat. "Someone killed her, Shea. I'm sure you can understand now why I had to come out here to establish your whereabouts for last night. The time of death has been estimated somewhere between seven and ten o'clock, but you didn't hear that from me, right?"

"Right," Shea murmured, nodding numbly.

"Now, how about you go grab your laptop and show me the time stamp for your blog post."

Shea stood, moving slowly toward the door. "Yeah, of course I can do that," she said, feeling dazed. She pulled the door open and caught Seth's gaze, her heart on her sleeve. "Seth, you don't really think that I had anything to do with this woman's murder, do you? I didn't even know the vet clinic had a lab."

"I'm just doing my job, Shea," Seth replied, betraying no emotion.

Shea nodded and went inside, the back of her eyelids stinging with unshed tears.

CHAPTER FOUR

After Seth verified that she had indeed been writing her blog post when she said she had, Shea showered and dressed quickly in clothing that would be presentable enough to wear to the sheriffs' department to give her voluntary statement. Seth had seemed satisfied enough with her alibi, but Shea was determined not to leave a single shred of doubt as to her whereabouts when Chelsea Russell was killed. She wanted it duly recorded and on an official record.

Though Shea was embarrassed at her own thoughts, she had to admit that she was also a bit peeved at whoever had called to report her little spit spat with Chelsea. Yes, they'd had words, but to make the leap from a bit of snark to murder was ridiculous.

The parking lot at the sheriff's department was fairly empty when Shea arrived and she realized that she had completely forgotten that it was Sunday after Seth had dropped his bombshell on her day. She checked in at the front desk and waited, tapping her foot and glancing at her watch more than once. Funny how time seemed to drag when one had to face an uncomfortable situation. She just wanted to get it over with and go back to her ordinary life.

One of the deputies that Shea recognized, but didn't actually know, came to the waiting room and led her back to a small office where he sat across the table from her with a notebook and a small recording device.

"Thank you for coming to the sheriff's department to give your voluntary statement in the matter of Chelsea Russell, deceased," he began, mechanically. "I have a few questions for you regarding this matter. First, please state your name, age, and current address."

Shea stared at him for a moment, then did as he asked, despite the fact that he spoke in a disinterested monotone and hadn't yet glanced up from his notebook.

"Thank you, Ms. Beaumont. Did you argue with Chelsea Russell yesterday at the farmer's market in front of your house?"

"Okay, wow. So I guess we're just jumping right in," Shea said, brows raised. "Fine. It wasn't exactly an argument. Chelsea was unreasonably angry with me. She assumed that I was mistreating my goats based on the prescription she brought out for me from Dr. Bev." Shea shrugged.

"And what was that prescription for?" the deputy asked.

"An infection. One of my goats delivered triplets and was very sore from nursing them. Apparently, the poor nanny's teats were raw from so much suckling, and the germs got in there and wreaked havoc," Shea said. "By the way, I didn't catch your name." She smiled, but when the deputy looked up at her, there was definitely no reciprocation. With his heavy Okie accent, she thought he might just say that his name was Deputy Dog, and she nearly giggled.

"Deputy Mayes. Are you mistreating the goat?" he asked flatly.

"No, of course not. Not at all," Shea replied, frowning.

"But the victim just assumed that you were?"

"Yes. Chelsea threw the bag with the ointment in it at me over the counter at my farmstand. She saw the goat milk products that I had for sale and made nasty comments about how I must be using the goats like machines or something."

"Did her accusation make you angry?" Mayes asked, in the same monotone. Shea began to wonder if the man was capable of emotion or expression.

"Yes, I was mad. I tried to reassure her that I wasn't mistreating them, but she wouldn't stop talking long enough to listen," Shea said, her blood beginning to simmer at the mere memory of the encounter.

"And later on you tracked her down at the veterinarian's office to explain it to her," the deputy stated.

"No, I did not," Shea said, her gaze landing on the top of his head as he wrote, eyes glued to the notebook. "I didn't go anywhere last night."

"But you did have more to say about it," Deputy Mayes finally looked her in the eye. "Your entire living depends on how your farm runs. So if the local vet tech runs around accusing you of mistreating your animals, that might cause you some real problems, right?"

Shea nodded. "It could. But I don't think the problems would be any worse than they would from her declaring it in the middle of the farmer's market on the busiest day."

"So, you wanted to get a little revenge on her, then?"

"Oh that's ridiculous. I wanted no such thing," Shea said. "I'd made up my mind to mention it to Dr. Beverly the next time I saw her, though. If I had to, I'd simply start going to another vet."

"But then you decided last night that you just couldn't wait, did't you? So you got into your car and drove into town and stopped by the vet clinic to see if you could find her there."

Shea stared at him, one eyebrow raised. Her twins, Chris and Carrie knew when they saw that look that a line had been crossed, and consequences were likely on the way.

"You're not listening very well, Deputy. I told you that I never left my house last night," Shea insisted.

"And I didn't need to go to see Dr. Bev. She'll be coming out to my house on Tuesday morning to take a look at the goat herself."

"You think she'll be able to confirm that?" Mayes drawled, a skeptical look on his face.

"She certainly should. I made the appointment a few days ago. In fact, I'd be delighted to wait right here while you go check," Shea said, glancing pointedly at the door.

The deputy stood and left the room without another word, the leather of his gun belt creaking with his every step.

Shea examined the small box of a windowless room that she'd been left in while he was gone, feeling her ire build. She'd merely defended herself during the interaction with Chelsea Russell, who had been clearly willing, if not actively trying, to provoke her. And while she was sad that the woman had been killed, she was beyond annoyed that she'd been dragged into the mess.

Sitting back in her horrifically uncomfortable metal folding chair, Shea folded her arms and rested one ankle on the top of the opposite knee. It was in this position that Mayes found her when he abruptly opened the door and strode back into the room.

"We're done here, Ms. Beaumont," he announced, his eyes as devoid of emotion as his tone.

"That's it? That's all you have to say?" Shea challenged, putting both feet firmly on the floor and sitting up ramrod straight in her chair.

"Don't leave town," the deputy replied, holding the door open and inclining his head to direct her to exit.

"Why would you say that?" Shea asked, not moving from her chair and drilling him with a glare. "Police only say that when they suspect you of something. Am I a suspect here?"

"Do you plan to leave town?" Mayes sounded bored.

"No, but that's not my point. You need to tell me if I'm being suspected of something," Shea replied.

"You're on a list of people who might have had a motive to kill Chelsea Russell," the deputy said. "And I can't remove you from that list just yet."

"How about you let me know who's on that list so I can clear my name faster," Shea suggested, her words dripping so much fake honey that the deputy probably gained weight.

"I think you know the answer to that," Mayes replied, using the toe of his shoe to tap down the rubber-ended door stop so that he didn't have to hold it open any longer. "You can see yourself out."

Shea walked back through the office and headed for her car. It felt worse than odd to walk by the closed door of Seth's office. It hurt, but she couldn't focus on that – she had things of grave importance to focus on at the moment. Part of her wanted to believe that this whole process was all just a formality, but her gut told her that she needed to do a little bit of digging herself just to make sure that she didn't wind up being unjustly accused. She was pretty sure that would be a relationship-ender with Seth. And things had been going so well.

CHAPTER FIVE

"I can't believe he suspects you." Trish's indignance was evident, even over the phone as Shea drove back to the farm. "Who was the little pipsqueak anyway? And why weren't you speaking with Andrea or Seth?"

"Well, I'm not exactly an expert on police procedure, but I'm guessing that it could be some kind of conflict of interest to have a statement taken by someone who was a friend or a dating partner," Shea said dryly. "I think they threw the meanest yahoo that happened to be on duty my way, too. He wasn't exactly a scintillating conversationalist. I have no idea what his first name is, but his last name is Mayes."

"Oh geez…it was Brian Mayes," Trish said, letting out what sounded like an exasperated sigh. "That boy's still wet behind the ears and he's determined to be a lifer, so he's out there being Tommy Tough Guy to prove himself."

"A lifer?" Shea repeated.

"Yeah, you know. A lifelong member of law enforcement. He's a piece of work. We can only hope that he takes it down a notch when he's had more experience," Trish said.

"Oh great, he sounds like the perfect one to be handling a murder case," Shea muttered.

"Awww…it's not as bad as all that, so keep your chin up, hon. Brian isn't running the case, he's just pinch-hitting for a very love-compromised sheriff," Trish teased.

"Don't you throw the L word around like that," Shea warned. "You're right, though. I guess I shouldn't be freaking out just yet. You and I both know that I had nothing to do with Chelsea Russell's death," Shea said, thinking aloud.

"But, on the other hand, I don't exactly see anyone besides me rushing to your defense either," Trish mused. "What are you going to do?"

Shea sighed. "I was going to say that I'm going to get home, go upstairs to take a nap, and get all of this mess out of my head," she replied. "But what I'm actually going to do is find out more about Chelsea Russell. Obviously, someone out there wanted to hurt her."

"Bless your heart, I really doubt it," Trish said. "Chelsea was the 'It' girl about a dozen years ago. And she still is a little bit, even now."

"I'm sorry…the what girl?" Shea asked.

"You know, the 'It' girl - homecoming queen, prom queen, the head cheerleader that everyone loves," Trish replied. "No one expected her to become a doctor or a lawyer or anything, but she was admired by pretty much everybody. I think she still is. She married her high school sweetheart and settled down on his mama's farm, then went to the technical college for a year, and studied under Dr. Bev after that."

"Peachy," Shea said, shaking her head. "I think I have my work cut out for me."

"Honestly, I can't think of anyone who would want to hurt her," Trish said.

"Aside from me," Shea added.

"Girl, you know better than that," Trish replied.

"I don't mean that you believe I did anything to her, just that I'm the only one who *appears* to have had a reason to do something," Shea said.

"That we know of. Listen, sweetie, I agree that it doesn't look good," Trish said. "But I don't think any reasonable person could believe that the tiny fuss you two raised at the market on Saturday morning would give you enough of a reason to murder her. If that was the case, you would have had it in for Helen Porter over a year ago." She chuckled.

"Thanks…I think," Shea said, laughing softly. "But another thing in my favor is that Chelsea clearly was holding some sort of grudge against me. She was the aggressive one who came out here and threw the prescription for the goats across the counter at me.

Not the other way around. I had even saved some of my best veggies for her."

"Right? I feel like she was already keyed up about something," Trish agreed. "Who gets that upset over something that is absolutely none of their business to start with? I mean, she had no idea what that ointment was for. Makes me wonder, because it doesn't seem like that kind of overreaction would be a part of her normal personality."

"I wouldn't think that she'd be so universally admired if she was that reactionary," Shea replied. "Maybe there was something in her life that made her upset before she even came out here."

"I don't know a whole lot about her family, but there's gotta be someone who does know," Trish mused.

Shea thought quietly for a long moment as she slowed the Jeep and pulled into her driveway.

Maybe Chelsea Russell was some kind of animal rights activist. But she knew that Dr. Bev's clinic could and would put down an animal if necessary. Surely an activist wouldn't work for a clinic with that policy.

And what if that was part of the issue? Chelsea could have expressed strong views that enraged someone along the way. Farmers who raised animals for a living respected them and sometimes even loved them. They might not take kindly to someone who called them out for doing what sometimes had to be done.

"I'm definitely going to look into this woman and find out a little more about her," Shea said. "I don't have a clue what I'm looking for, but if whatever I find helps to clear my name, it'll be totally worth it."

"Just be careful," Trish warned. "If someone was angry enough with her to…do what they did, and they find out you're digging into it, you could put yourself in a whole world of hurt. And it's not just you that you have to worry about now."

Carrie's face flashed through Shea's mind, making her catch her breath. "I know," she said, eventually. "But I also know my daughter well enough to know that she won't stand for sitting still and doing nothing."

"Too much like her mama," Trish said dryly.

Shea chuckled. "Yeah, I guess so. I'll be careful, I promise," she said. "But I can't guarantee that I won't be nosy."

Trish snorted with laughter but repeated her concerns before she hung up. Shea parked and went into the house, lost in thought.

"What happened? Were they mean? I already did the chores and made a late lunch, so don't worry about that, just tell me everything," Carrie demanded, hugging her mother as soon as she got in the door.

"But did you remember the wine?" Shea teased.

"Already poured." Carrie gestured to the dining room.

"Okay, I was actually kidding about that, but now that I think about it, it sounds like a great idea. Let's sit down and I'll fill you in. I only want one glass of wine though. I think better when I'm in the garden, so I'm going to get my hands in the dirt after lunch," Shea said, following her daughter into the dining room, where a lavish charcuterie board lunch had been set out.

"Have I ever told you that you're amazing?" Shea breathed, taking in the feast.

"Once. When I was five, but it's good to know nothing's changed," Carrie teased. "Now sit! We need to eat so you can tell me everything. I've been dying to hear."

When she said 'now sit,' Samson, who had just wandered into the dining room, obediently stopped in his tracks and sat.

"Good boy." Carrie smiled at him and tossed him a carrot stick. "Now, spill it," she told her mother. "Not you," she said to Samson, grinning. He cocked his head at her.

After lunch was over and the food was put away, Shea went upstairs to slip into a pair of loose-fitting pants and a long-sleeved t-shirt to protect her from bugs, sunburn, and anything else Mother Nature wanted to throw at her, while Carrie took care of the dishes.

The late afternoon air, as the sun began to slip behind the big barn was chilly, but not unpleasant as Shea and Carrie headed for the largest greenhouse.

Moments later, they stood inside the garden shed with two trays of tomato seedlings, each, and, donning their gardening gloves and a couple of handheld shovels and headed out to the west field.

With a little help from her friends, Shea had learned how to operate a small garden tiller, which she used between the rows of growing plants to keep the weeds at a minimum and to prepare the soil for any planting that she'd planned to do within a week or so.

Shea took one row and Carrie took the next, so that they could either work silently side by side, or chat about how to proceed in light of recent events. They set the trays of plants to the side and started digging into the dirt, carving out small holes for each plant. Working at exactly the same rate, without even realizing it, Shea and Carrie carefully removed the tender plants from the trays and set them down gently into their new homes, packing the earth firmly around each one.

After finishing with the first tray, Shea paused to study the dirt, taking off her glove for a moment to appreciate the richness of it as she sifted it through her fingers, and smiled when she glanced up to see Carrie studying her with a soft look on her face.

"I can't help myself," she admitted, chuckling.

Carrie nodded. "No, I totally get it. Even the smell of it is somehow…compelling," she agreed.

"It totally is. Now, get back to digging, we have some important thinking to do and digging helps the process," Shea teased.

"Yes ma'am!" Carrie said, in a mock Oklahoma accent, saluting her mother with a garden-gloved hand.

It took another hour to plant the remainder of the trays, but when they were finished, Shea stood to survey their work and smiled at the progress. Despite the emotional turmoil of the day, they had accomplished something, and it felt great. Unfortunately, with the gardening done, her ever-active mind and imagination had nothing else to focus on, aside from the unpleasant reality of her situation.

"How on earth could they possibly be looking at me as a suspect?" she blurted, as she and Carrie stashed their equipment back in the garden shed.

"I was just wondering the same thing," Carrie admitted. "Like what could have even been your motive? Makes me wonder who reported you."

"Yeah, I wondered about that too," Shea replied. "I guess there are probably still people around here who view me as an outsider, and after the background

Trish gave me on Chelsea, she was one of the town's folk heroes. It's so frustrating. I've been busting my behind to make a good life and reputation for myself since I set foot in this town. What more do I have to do to prove myself?"

"Well, exonerating yourself might be a good place to start," Carrie suggested quietly.

Shea put an arm around her shoulders and gave her a hug.

CHAPTER SIX

Sunday evening Shea decided to spend the rest of the evening inside with the doors locked and the curtains drawn. She fought the temptation to shut her phone completely off but decided against that simply because she wanted her phone to keep track of her location, just in case someone else in the small town of Pawnee was murdered and the sheriff's department couldn't come up with a decent suspect.

She found it not only odd, but painful, that neither Seth nor Andrea had reached out to her. Not that they owed her anything, but neither of them had even texted to check in with her after she'd been questioned by Deputy Mayes.

"It's not about me, it's about the appearance of a conflict of interest," she murmured to herself, but the longer they remained silent, the more difficult it was for Shea to believe.

Wandering around her room while depressing thoughts whirled through her brain wasn't helping her to relax at all, so she came to an impulsive decision.

"Hey, Samson," she turned and addressed her faithful furry friend, who had been watching her pace back and forth, his head on his paws. He thumped his tail when she spoke to him. "You wanna go for a ride in the car?"

He was on his feet and at the bedroom door almost before she finished her sentence. Carrie was in the living room with her laptop when Shea came down the stairs, Samson close behind.

"So you decided to stop wearing a path in your carpet?" she teased, when Shea appeared.

"Yeah, driving myself crazy with what-ifs wasn't exactly productive, so I thought I'd get out of the house for a bit."

"Probably a good idea. Where are you going?" Carrie asked.

"Honestly, I'm probably going to go to the grocery store and get some snacks and a six pack of beer." Shea smiled wearily.

"Now you're talking. Want me to come with?" Carrie asked.

"Nah, I won't be gone long. I'll give Samson some quality time," Shea replied, reaching down to scratch between the dog's ears.

"Sounds good. I'm working on an article about chicken feed for Agriculture Focus magazine, so I'll be ready for beer, snacks, and a good movie when you get back."

"Chicken feed?" Shea's brows rows.

"Yep. I've been doing research. It turns out that their feed can impact everything from egg size to lifespan to feather shininess," Carrie replied.

Shea's heart overflowed with pride. "Well, goodness knows we want our girls to have shiny feathers." She smiled.

"I know, right? Pretty and productive – can't beat it," Carrie said, chuckling.

"Yeah, can't wait to see Clarence strutting around when he figures out he has shiny feathers. See you soon. Pick out a movie for us to watch when I get back," Shea directed, heading to the door.

"You got it."

Carrie had returned to tapping on her laptop before Shea and Samson even reached the door. Shea got to the end of the driveway and realized that she might run into more hostility than she was prepared to deal with if she went into town, so she went right instead of left, and pulled into the parking lot of a small convenience store that surrounded the campgrounds on the way to Lake Pawnee.

It may have been her overactive imagination, but Shea felt that every eye in the place was on her when she entered the little shop, so she hurried straight to the coolers in the back, snagged a six pack of her favorite stout, and grabbed random bags of snacks on her way to the checkout counter.

"Interesting choice for a lady," the young cashier commented, chomping on her gum, when Shea placed the box of bottled beer on the counter with her snacks. "Or did you pick that up for your man?"

Shea sighed, reminding herself that she was fully capable of picking her battles, and pulled her debit card out of her wallet. She smiled at the gum chomper and slid her card into the card reader. "Nope, it's actually for me," she said. "I like beer that you can't see through."

"You can't see through that?" the cashier peered at the six pack.

"No. It looks just like you poured a Coca Cola."

"Bet it don't taste like no Coca Cola." The young woman smiled, revealing a gold capped incisor that somehow fascinated Shea.

"No, it definitely doesn't. Tastes better than most beers though," Shea replied.

"Well, you enjoy it then," the cashier handed her a receipt.

"Thank you, I will." She picked up the six pack and her bag of snacks and headed back out into the evening. Samson wagged his tail, grinning his delighted doggie grin when she got back into the Jeep. "Oh buddy, I'm so sorry. I got out of there so fast that I forgot to get you a treat."

Samson replied by giving her a giant slurp right across the cheek. "Ewww. I'll make something special for you before the movie. I just can't take anymore of humanity right now." Shea sighed, glancing back at the cashier, who was currently flirting with a pot-bellied man in a cowboy hat.

Pulling out onto the highway, she couldn't wait to get back home, and when she walked in, Carrie had already finished her article and selected a movie. Samson bounded over to where she sat on the couch and proceeded to try and curl up on her lap.

"Hey, ya big baby!" she exclaimed, giggling. "Where'd you get the idea that you were a lap dog?"

"He's choosing you as his favorite at the moment because I forgot to get him a doggie treat," Shea explained, smiling at the dog's antics. He'd been quiet in the car after his initial greeting, seeming to pick up on Shea's mood.

"Lucky me. You okay?" Carrie asked, tousling Samson's ears while looking carefully at her mother. The girl missed nothing.

"Yeah, I will be. Eventually. I suppose. Hey, do you mind getting the snacks ready while I change and grab my laptop?"

"Can do. You gonna do some digging before the movie?" Carrie asked, snapping her fingers to let Samson know to vacate her lap so that she could move.

"You know me too well." Shea smiled again.

Carrie shrugged. "It's what I'd do."

By the time Shea came back into the living room, Carrie had put the junk food that she'd brought home in small bowls and had augmented their evening snack with cheese slices, tender chunks of leftover chicken, fresh grapes, olives, and some of Shea's homemade bread and butter pickles. Two beers rested in a giant salad bowl filled with ice, and Carrie had lit the fireplace.

"Young lady, I wish you'd lived here back when I first arrived. It's nice to be taken care of every once in a while," Shea said, taking it all in.

"Yeah, sometimes I wish that too," Carrie confessed, with a shy smile. "I missed our hanging out times."

"Same."

"I poured your beer when I heard you coming down the stairs, and I know you can't drink a six pack by yourself, so I poured one for me too. Great choice – it's delish," Carrie approved.

"Thank you. At least I can do something right," Shea replied, settling down onto the couch and tucking her feet under her.

She opened her laptop and searched for Chelsea Russell's name, nearly choking on a grape when the first articles that popped up were a series on her recent death. Scanning the first one, she swallowed hard after reading about what had actually happened. Chelsea had been strangled and the rather graphic nature of the details in the article made her close the laptop, put it down next to her on the couch, and take a swig of beer.

"Let me guess, news about the murder," Carrie said quietly. Shea nodded and took another sip. "You don't have to do this right now, you know. We can watch the movie and get into research in the morning."

Shea shook her head. "There's too much to do in the morning."

"Curiosity killed the cat, you know," Carrie warned, munching on an olive.

"That's why we have a dog." Shea smiled faintly as Carrie groaned and tossed a pillow at her.

"Hey, don't spill the beer," Shea protested. "I'm gonna need it to do this research."

"I can look too, if you'd like," Carrie offered.

Shea shook her head. "Nope. I just have to do this myself, so it doesn't drive me nuts."

"Fair enough. But tell me if you find something interesting."

After a few more nibbles of snacks, Shea reopened her computer and opened a new tab, going to social media platforms. She finally found an account with the name "Chelsea Anne" and started clicking through the photos in the account.

"What are you looking at?" Carrie startled her by asking.

"A social media account. I was looking through Chelsea's pictures."

"Well, I guess that explains why you're crying," Carrie said, giving her mother a sympathetic look.

Shea's hand went to her cheek, and she was surprised to find it damp. "She had two sisters," she murmured. "They all look so much alike."

Carrie scooted over and put her head on Shea's shoulder, looking at the photos as her mother continued to scroll.

"Billy…that's obviously her husband. They looked so cute together. Looks like they started dating in grade school, they're so young in some of these," Carrie commented.

Shea nodded and kept scrolling. "At least she didn't leave any kids behind," she said sadly. Chelsea Russell would never know the joy of having a child.

"That does it." Shea blew out a sigh. "I don't just want to clear my name anymore; I want to find justice for Chelsea. She may have been mean to me, but she had what looked like a great life, with people who loved her, and someone stole that."

"I agree," Carrie said, as Shea finished her bottle of beer and rose to get a second one.

"You want another?" she called over her shoulder on the way to the kitchen.

"No, still working on this one." Carrie held up her half empty bottle.

When Shea came back, she searched for Billy's name on social media, scrolling through his photos when she found him.

"Well, there are no favorite books listed on his profile, but he sure did like his action movies," Shea commented. "And his action movie stars, apparently."

Billy Russell was an oil rig worker. Shea was curious about the job so she looked for more information about it. Carrie glanced over and gave her a look.

"So, is knowing what oil rig workers do going to help you find justice?" she asked.

Shea sighed and closed her laptop. "I'm just spinning my wheels. I don't even know what I'm looking for."

Samson came over and rested his head on her knee, gazing up at her with adoration.

"I think he's telling you it's time to take a break and watch the movie," Carrie said, reaching over to stroke the dog's silky ears.

"I think he's right," Shea admitted, smiling at her golden boy. "Movie, then bed. Tomorrow is a new day and we'll make it a new start."

"Everything looks better in the light of day," Carrie said.

"I sure hope so." Shea sighed.

CHAPTER SEVEN

After the movie, which had been a wonderfully irreverent comedy that she didn't have to pay much attention to in order to enjoy, Shea made the decision that she wouldn't be opening open up her farm stand in the morning. It was still early enough in the season that being closed a couple of days each week wouldn't be an issue at all.

This time of year, even the weather could cause her to close down on any given day. If any of her fellow vendors wanted to open for the day, they'd be more than welcome to, but she secretly hoped that no one would show. She'd text Trish about it so that her bestie could get the word out.

Shea turned the lights out just after eleven, hugged Carrie, and headed up the stairs to bed.

Unfortunately, despite a full tummy and a beer and a half, sleep didn't come easily. It was sometime after midnight, before Shea finally fell asleep, and her dreams were filled with dark images of the veterinary clinic and her imagination's version of what the death scene must have looked like. She startled awake sometime before dawn with the sheets pressing against her throat and panicked briefly before realizing that she was perfectly safe and sound, at home in her bed.

Shea pushed the covers back and swung her feet over the side of the bed, adrenaline still crashing through her. Samson sprang to his feet and barked.

"It's okay, buddy," Shea soothed him, patting his head on her way to the bathroom. "Go back to sleep."

She headed down the hall to the upstairs bathroom, then pulled on her robe and decided to go downstairs for a drink of water. Samson, being the sleepy good boy that he was, remained obediently upstairs at the foot of her bed.

After downing a glass of water in a few swallows, Shea was dismayed to find that she wasn't the slightest bit sleepy, but since it was just after four in the morning, it seemed a bit too early to start her day. Thanks to the early spring cold snap, Carrie had turned on two warming lamps in the chicken coop, and after a restless few hours of sleep, Shea wasn't exactly excited to go out into the cold anyway.

The thought of going upstairs and trying to get back to sleep held no appeal, either, so Shea leaned against the kitchen sink, trying to figure out what to do.

"Well, Chelsea, since you kept me up all night, I guess I'd better get working on finding your killer," Shea mumbled, heading to her office and opening her laptop.

She decided to take another look at Chelsea's social media profiles again and found the names of, and some information about, Chelsea's sisters. Erica Marshall was the first sister that Shea was able to identify. She was a mother of three and appeared in many of Chelsea's vacation photos. Jessica was the other sister – Shea confirmed that by looking at her profile and discovering that she had listed Chelsea and Erica as her sisters.

"This is all well and good, but I still don't know anything else about you, Chelsea," she murmured, looking over the photos for both sisters. There was nothing at all in any of the sisters' photos that pointed toward Chelsea having any sort of enemies or that would indicate any reason that someone had a reason to kill her.

What she did find were tons photos of the sisters with their respective families. Both Jessica and Erica had children. Shea wasn't absolutely sure about the birth order of the sisters, but it seemed like Chelsea might've been the middle sister, between the younger one, Jessica, and the older one, Erica.

Many of their shared photos were of the three sisters standing together, smiling, in front of a beach, or a boat, or another body of water. Chelsea's husband, Billy, appeared in several other photos, but, though it was clear that there was a close relationship among the sisters, what wasn't clear was why Billy wasn't in any of the most recent photos.

Her curiosity piqued, Shea entered Billy Russell's name again and checked through his photos more closely on both social media sites that she'd used for her research. She found Billy in a few photos with other guys who looked more like his good buddies rather than brothers or other relatives. He also appeared in several photos of fishing and hunting trips.

"Interesting, but not helpful in the least." Shea sighed, rubbing her temples. "I need coffee."

She returned to the kitchen and made coffee, leaning against the counter and staring into space while it brewed. As soon as the ancient coffeemaker began its final gurgles, indicating that it was done, Shea poured herself a giant mug, topped it off with fresh cream, and headed back to her office.

She began searching again with the oldest photos that she could find on Billy's profile, scanning through numerous shots of Billy in high school along with a smiling Chelsea in her green and white cheerleader uniform at his side, grinning as though they hadn't a care in the world.

"The good ole days," Shea murmured sadly.

She found a couple of pictures of an older couple whom she guessed might be Billy's parents and examined a photo of him standing between them that caught her eye. They were posing outside a one-story building with lots of windows. "Russell's Diner" was written in an old-fashioned script on the glass behind them.

"Russell's Diner," she said, placing her cursor over the photo. If the diner had been tagged in the photo, the location would pop up as her cursor hovered over it. As luck would have it, no one had tagged the diner, so Shea closed out of the social media site and typed the name of the diner into the search engine.

"Bingo," she said, her heart rate accelerating. The diner was located just west of Lake Pawnee, south of town. Shea checked out their hours and planned to show up for coffee right after they opened.

CHAPTER EIGHT

"Hey, want to go to breakfast?" Shea asked Carrie when she trudged down the stairs a bit before six.

"Shouldn't we be getting out there to feed the animals and get the veggies ready for the market?" Carrie asked, clearly confused.

"I fed the animals, milked the goats, and did the rest of the chores aside from setting up for the market. We're staying closed today and you and I are going on a little field trip," Shea announced, glad to finally have a lead, even if it would likely turn out to be nothing.

"You're staying closed?" Carrie's brows rose. "What are you up to, and why do I have the distinct feeling that your breakfast invitation has a hidden motive?"

"You are definitely my daughter," Shea said, grinning. "Yes, guilty as charged. We're going to breakfast at Russell's Diner, near Lake Pawnee, today."

"Russell as in Chelsea Russell?" Carrie suddenly seemed wide awake.

"More like as in Billy Russell. His parents' diner, actually. I found out about it on social media this morning," Shea replied.

"Wait, this morning? You fed the animals, milked the goats, did the chores, and still had time to find an obscure reference to a diner on social media? What time did you get up, Mom?" Carrie frowned.

"Four thirty-ish." Shea waved a hand dismissively.

"We didn't get to bed until after eleven…"

"I know, and I tossed and turned until after midnight before I could get to sleep," Shea replied.

"I'm driving," Carrie announced.

"I knew you would."

Russell's Diner was an older, but well-kept aluminum-clad building located in the middle of a city block and was surrounded on three sides with parking spaces. Shea pulled opened the front door and was immediately engulfed by the intoxicating smell of bacon and freshly-brewed coffee.

"Whoa," Carrie whispered from behind her.

Entering the diner was like stepping back in time. From the worn, but spotless, black and white tiles on the floor to the Naugahyde upholstered booths and red bar stools, the interior looked like a magazine ad from the 1950s. The servers were dressed in pale pink dresses from a bygone era, and most had their hair done up in fifties style and wore costume jewelry straight out of I Love Lucy. Shea was gazing at a poster of Elvis Presley that hung over one of the booths when a server approached.

"Mornin' y'all. Breakfast for two?" she asked.

"Yes, please," Shea replied, so charmed by the experience that she nearly forgot that she was on a mission. She and Carrie followed the woman to a small booth that had a mini jukebox on the tabletop, next to the window. Even the menus had fifties graphics.

"What can I get y'all to drink this mornin'?" the server asked, pulling an order pad and pen from her apron pocket.

"Coffee, please," Shea and Carrie said, in unison. The server chuckled and promised she'd be right back.

"Mom, have you seen this menu? They've got every kind of comfort food you could possibly imagine," Carrie breathed, wide-eyed.

"Might as well go big or go home," Shea said, picking up her menu.

The server was back in minutes with a coffee pot, a pitcher of cream, an actual sugar bowl, and two heavy mugs on a tray that she balanced on one hand. She set a mug down in front of each of them and poured the coffee, then placed the cream and sugar on the table.

"Y'all decide what you're wanting for breakfast today?" she asked, tucking the tray under her arm and whipping out her order pad like the pro that she obviously was.

Shea's stomach growled, and they all laughed.

"Well, based on that reaction, I'd suggest our breakfast sampler," the server said. "It comes with a half order of biscuits and gravy, your choice of eggs, four strips of country bacon, and a short stack of pancakes with whipped butter and warm maple syrup."

"That's literally every breakfast food that I'm craving right now," Shea said. "I'll take it, with eggs scrambled and bacon extra crispy, please."

"You got it," the server beamed and took her menu. "How 'bout you, hon?" she asked Carrie.

"I'm torn between the cinnamon roll pancakes and the triple berry french toast," Carrie said, as Shea stared at her in shock.

"Well, I'd be happy to get you a half order of both, if you'd like. That would also come with fried potatoes and onions, eggs, and your choice of meat." The server's pen was poised over her pad.

"Half of both sounds great, and I'll take scrambled eggs and bacon, please," Carrie said.

"You want yours extra crispy too?" the server asked.

"Yes, please."

"Like mother, like daughter, am I right?" the server said. "Alright ladies, I'll be back in a flash with that for you."

Shea grinned at Carrie

"What?" Carrie asked.

"How are you even going to eat half of that food you ordered?" Shea chuckled.

"I'm a farm girl now – my appetite is better." Carrie shrugged. "Is it just me, or does this place seem like we've walked into an episode of The Twilight Zone?"

"It kind of does, but in the best possible way," Shea replied. "Did you notice, every server is busy, and the cooks over there behind the counter are too, but like…no one seems to be in a rush?"

"Must be a happy place to work," Carrie mused.

In what seemed like seconds, their server returned with a large tray of food in one hand and a portable stand to set it on in the other. She cheerfully loaded up the table with plate after plate of luscious looking food.

"Oh, my," Shea said. "It looks like enough food for an army."

"Challenge accepted." Carrie grinned.

The waitress chuckled and set a syrup decanter down in front of Shea's coffee mug. "Can I bring you a glass of ice cold orange juice as well?" she asked. "I should have told you that it comes with the sampler."

"Go big or go home," Carrie reminded her.

"Then, actually, yes," Shea replied. "I appreciate it."

"You got it. I'll be right back with that," the server said with a wink.

Shea smiled, then, after the server left, she and Carrie dug in with gusto. An older couple, whom she recognized from their photos, came in, followed by a younger man, who also looked familiar. Shea didn't know whether to feel worried or excited at the sudden appearance of the Russells and their son, Billy.

The trio slid into the large corner booth across the aisle from Shea and Carrie. Shea gave Carrie a meaningful look, then shifted her eyes to the right. Carrie casually glanced over, then looked back at her mother and nodded imperceptibly.

"When is your next shift?" Mrs. Russell asked Billy. Their booth was close enough that Shea could hear their conversation perfectly, without having to strain even a bit.

"Depends on when they need me, but probably tomorrow night," Billy replied. He picked up his coffee and took a sip.

"Have you heard anything else from the police?" Billy's father asked.

"Can we just not speak of this right now?" his mother said sharply. "It's bad enough that it even happened at all. Does it have to ruin my breakfast too?"

"Her death is public knowledge, Mama," Billy said, sighing. "Everybody knew Chelsea."

"You didn't answer my question," Billy's father addressed him again. "Do the police want anything else from you?"

"No, not as far as I know," Billy said, staring into his coffee mug.

"Well, do they at least have a suspect in mind?" Bill Sr. persisted.

"They've questioned me and a few other people from what I've heard, Dad. But they don't have any better idea what happened to her than I do." He shook his head. "I feel like they'd just love it if I broke down and confessed. I mean, that's how it usually happens, right? It's always the husband or the ex, am I right?"

"Hush now, son," Mrs. Russell said, before turning to look directly at Shea. "Please disregard what my son is saying. He really isn't wanted by the police." Her smile was a rictus of dismay.

Shea gave her a compassionate smile and glanced at Billy. "I'm very sorry about your wife," she said before she could think better of it. Carrie kicked her under the table.

"Is it true? Does everyone in these parts really know about Chelsea's death?" Mrs. Russell whispered to her son, looking horrified.

"No, no, ma'am," Shea blurted, throwing more words out with careless abandon. "I only know about it because I'm one of the people the sheriff questioned."

Carrie cleared her throat loudly, but Shea was only peripherally aware of it as she mentally kicked herself for her loose tongue.

"Excuse me, but what in the Sam Heck is going on here?" Bill Russell Sr. demanded, his steely blue gaze pinning Shea to her seat. "What's your angle lady?

Are you some kind of reporter? Did you just come here to poke around for a good news story?"

"No, I'm not a reporter," Shea replied. "I'm literally one of the people that the sheriff's department questioned."

"Why would they wanna talk to you?" Billy asked, his eyes narrowing.

"Because I had a small disagreement with Chelsea at the farmer's market on Saturday morning," Shea replied. "Dr. Bev had asked her to deliver some ointment for one of my goats. Chelsea misunderstood the purpose of the ointment, and it made her upset."

"How could she possibly have misunderstood that," Billy challenged. "She's worked for Dr. Bev for ten years."

"She assumed that because I needed it to treat my nanny goat for an infection, that I must have been overmilking the poor thing just to make products from her milk, but the truth is, the nanny just had triplets, and that's what had caused the irritation that gave her the infection," Shea explained. "Anyway, we had a very public disagreement about it at the farmers market and I suppose somebody thought that it might've given me enough of a motive to…do something about it," she finished as tactfully as she could.

"Did it?" Bill Sr. asked her. "Because if you're some sicko who came here to make another scene, I can assure you that it won't go well for you."

Shea's brows rose. She didn't take kindly to threats, but she also understood that she was dealing with a grieving family and responded accordingly. "No," she replied. "I am most certainly not a sicko and definitely not a murderer. I had nothing to do with her death. Believe me, if that little exchange had been enough to push me over the edge, my former husband would have been dead and gone some time ago."

Mrs. Russell covered her mouth and giggled. Mr. Russell shot her what looked like a warning look. "Uh-huh. So you just happened to show up here for breakfast out of the blue? I don't recall ever seeing you around here before," he said.

"I came by here because I was curious about Chelsea's family, to be honest," Shea replied.

"Curious about us?" Billy gave her a puzzled look.

Shea nodded. "I wondered if you might have done it."

Carrie dropped her fork onto her plate and brought a hand to her forehead.

"So, you just decided to show up and ask if our son killed his wife?" Bill Sr. threw his napkin on the table in front of him, a vein on his forehead pulsing as his face went red.

"Ex-wife, Dad," Billy said, his tone resigned.

"No, of course not," Shea refrained from rolling her eyes, but it took every bit of her willpower. She'd dealt with bullying men before, her ex was a prime example, and Bill Sr. didn't intimidate her in the least. "But I was up all night wondering about her and why she was killed. Call me crazy but I feel like she deserves the justice of having her killer found. Maybe I should just go." Shea pushed her plate away and waved at their server.

"Maybe you should," Bill Sr. said, his teeth clenched.

"Absolutely not," Mrs. Russell said, giving her husband a look like the one he'd given her. "You just go right ahead and eat your breakfast, dear. If you're looking into the death of our daughter-in-law, have you found out anything that might be helpful?"

"I highly doubt it, Sylvia," Bill Sr. said. "And she was almost our *former* daughter-in-law. The papers had already been filed. I bet you didn't know that, did you?" he asked, turning back to Shea.

"No, but I'm not exactly surprised," Shea said.

"What makes you say that?" Billy asked, waving off the server who had come to refill the coffee cups.

"Your photos on social media," Shea replied. "I noticed that there were a lot of older photos of the two of you together, with each other's families and friends. Then, starting about a year ago, no more photos of the two of you were added. Is that when you started having problems?"

"You know who you ought to be asking about all that?" Billy said, his jaw set. "Beau Price, that's who."

"Who's Beau Price?" Shea asked, as Bill Sr. shook his head and wiped his forehead with a napkin.

"Well, you might say he's the type of person you don't mention in polite company," Sylvia Russell said primly. "Even the sound of his name turns my stomach."

"I think I'm getting the picture," Shea said quietly. "So when Chelsea met…him, things in your relationship went sour, right?" she asked Billy.

"When I found out about him is when things went sour," Billy corrected. "But that was a long time ago. If I was gonna go crazy and hurt my ex, it wouldn't have been that long after I found out about it."

"I can see why the police were interested in speaking to you about it, though," Shea said, thinking aloud.

"Good thing he has a solid alibi that his mother and I can vouch for," Bill Sr. said. "Along with about a hundred other people. What's your alibi look like?"

"Well, you might have to ask my daughter, my best friend, and my farm animals about that," Shea replied. "I was online writing a post for my blog and the sheriff has already verified that. What's your alibi?"

Bill's mouth worked and he turned an alarming shade of red. Shea braced herself, but it was his wife who spoke up first. "We were at a retirement dinner for Bill's former co-worker. Billy works for the same company now, so he came with us, and most of the people there know who he is," Sylvia explained. "And we were there until well past midnight."

"But your alibi is that you were writing? I thought you said you weren't a reporter," Bill growled, looking like a pressure cooker that was ready to blow.

"And I'll say it again, I'm not a reporter. I write a blog about the antics of the animals on my farm and the mishaps I've had learning how to become a market farmer," Shea shot back. "I'd be more apt to write about my cranky old rooster biting my dog on the hindquarters than about a murder."

"But you came here to check me out," Billy said. "You think of yourself as some kind of an investigator or something?"

Shea sighed deeply. "No." She slid out of the booth, stood, and pulled a twenty out of her purse, then took her last swig of coffee and set the empty cup down on the table with the twenty under it. "I'm nothing of the sort. I was just here to find out anything I could about who might have harmed an innocent young woman," she said.

"That might come in real handy if the cops decide that they need to have a second conversation with you, right? If there's someone else who can take the heat, it would be good to go in knowing that, now wouldn't it?" Bill Sr. said with a smirk.

Shea cocked her head to the side and raised an eyebrow at him. "Not if what I found out makes it look like I'm back to square one," she replied. "Because I haven't heard anything here that gets me any closer to finding out what happened to her."

"If that's what you think…maybe you ain't as bright as you think you are, lady," Bill Sr. replied.

CHAPTER NINE

Shea and Carrie rode toward home in relative silence as Shea processed the fact that she had met not only the husband of the woman who had been murdered, but both of his parents. All three had a less than stellar opinion of the deceased woman. But all three had solid alibis.

It did strike her as odd that Mrs. Russell was quick to add how late the three of them were at the retirement dinner. She made a mental note to check out more newspaper articles about the discovery of Chelsea's body. She couldn't remember if the time of death had been published or not. Then there was Beau Price.

"So…Beau Price," Carrie said, breaking the silence.

"Yeah, that's what I was just thinking about too," Shea replied.

"Chelsea took quite a bit of time to begin the divorce process. Do you think Beau might've gotten tired of her dragging her feet?" Carrie mused.

"She may have dragged her feet worse than we think," Shea replied.

"Huh?"

"When Bill Sr. talked about papers being filed, he never said who filed them. Chelsea may have wanted to have her cake and eat it too. It may have been Billy who filed for divorce."

"Meaning…?"

"Meaning that if Chelsea had been stringing Beau along, telling him that she'd filed for divorce, and he somehow found out that she hadn't…"

"He may have decided to make it unnecessary," Carrie finished the thought. "Does that make sense though? If he wanted her to get a divorce so that she could be with him, why would he kill her?"

"Well, someone killed her, and those three have an alibi. Maybe they'd had a fight after Beau found out." Shea shook her head in frustration.

"Bill Sr. seemed awfully angry," Carrie commented. "You handled him well though. Years of practice?"

Shea took a breath. "Sweetie, I'm so sorry about saying that about your dad in front of you. It was a horrible thing for me to do. I was just so mad at that…"

"Bully? Mr. Russell definitely was a bully, and don't think for a moment that I was so oblivious that I didn't see that Dad was like that to you too," Carrie said.

Stunned, Shea didn't know quite how to react. Tears sprung to her eyes.

"I never want you and Chris to feel like you have to take sides," she whispered, swallowing past the lump in her throat.

"We're not. We love you, we love Dad. That doesn't mean that we don't recognize how awful he was to you most of the time. We saw it. The divorce was kind of a relief, actually. I mean, it's not like we didn't like our home life – you were both always loving with us. Well, I mean, Dad was gone most of the time, but we always knew you loved us," Carrie confessed.

"And we always will, CareBear."

"You haven't called me that in years. I like it," Carrie said with a smile.

Before Shea could reply, her phone rang. Frustrated, she hit the button on the Jeep's dash to put the call on speaker.

"Where have you been?" Trish demanded, the second she answered.

"To a diner on the other side of the county," Shea replied, still rattled by her daughter's revelations. "Why?"

"Because I've been trying to reach you for over an hour. Seth is looking for you," Trish said.

"First of all, leaving to go to a diner south of town to have breakfast isn't like I was fleeing from the law," Shea said. "I must've left my phone in the car."

"Well, you certainly don't have to check in with me, girl," Trish replied. "But I was curious about where you went. You okay?"

"Yeah, I'm fine. Sorry, I didn't mean to snap at you – I didn't get much sleep last night. Why is the sheriff looking for me?" Shea asked.

"Girl, if there was any more ice in your tone *the sheriff* would have to get his parka just to talk to you. He stopped by your house to check on you, but he said you weren't home," Trish said.

"This morning?" Shea asked.

"Just a little bit ago. You might want to check your phone and see if he left you a message or anything."

"I'll probably call him when I get home," Shea said.

"You'll probably call him. Who are you and what have you done with Shea Beaumont?" Trish teased. "So, are you going to tell me about your trip to this diner? What did you find out? I know you didn't go out into the middle of nowhere just for the pancakes."

"Biscuits and gravy actually. What makes you think I had an ulterior motive?" Shea asked, chuckling.

"Because my biscuits and gravy are the best in all the land, hands down. If you had a hankering for that, you'd have been on my front porch at dawn. I'm guessing that maybe you were just trying to figure out if Billy Russell killed his wife," Trish replied.

"You know about the diner?"

"You're not the only one with a laptop, you know," Trish said. "I mean, I'm quite literally looking up the diner right now. It didn't take me long to narrow it down."

"They do have good food," Shea said. "I had the breakfast sampler. And the coffee was fresh."

"Well that's all very nice, but you better start spillin' the tea about what you found out quick, fast, and in a hurry."

Shea exhaled dramatically. "Oh fine, if you must know, I got a confession out of Billy, his father, and the fry cook."

"You're hilarious. Now spill. Don't make me drive over and wait for you."

Shea laughed. "Okay, okay, what I actually found out is that Billy and Chelsea split," Shea replied. "But they never got divorced."

"What?" Trish exclaimed. "That doesn't make any sense."

"Well, Billy told me that if I wanted to talk to someone about the questions I had I should check with a guy named Beau Price," Shea said. "Apparently when Billy found out that Chelsea took up with Beau is when their marriage started going bad."

"So, who is Beau, then? What did you find out about him?" Trish asked.

"Slow your roll, girl," Shea said. "As of right now, you know as much as I do."

"Good, that means that I can start looking him up before you even get home." Trish giggled wickedly. "So, what's your plan now?"

"Well, I guess I'm going to go home and call the sheriff to find out what he wanted," Shea said, the frost returning to her tone. "Do me a favor, okay?"

"You know it. Whatcha need?" Trish asked.

"If the reason that the sheriff stopped by was to haul me to jail for the murder of Chelsea Russell, promise me that you'll teach Carrie everything she needs to know to keep the farm running."

"Oh, stop it," Trish said. Shea knew her well enough that she could practically hear her eyes rolling. "I seriously doubt that's why Seth drove to your house."

"Why? Maybe he just came out in person so he could break it to me gently," Shea said.

"Break it to you gently that you're being arrested? How in the world would that be gentle?" Trish asked.

"I don't know," Shea grumbled. "But I guess I'm about to find out. I just passed his car." She watched in her rearview as the sheriff made a U-turn on the highway. He turned on his flashing lights as soon as he pulled in behind her.

"Is everything okay?" Trish asked.

"I guess I'll find out. It looks like I am being pulled over," Shea said with a sigh. "Don't forget to teach Carrie everything you taught me."

"As if I could ever forget," Trish said.

CHAPTER TEN

Shea pulled over on the shoulder as far as she could and rolled her window down. She pulled her wallet out of her purse and opened the glove box for her registration and insurance information, then waited while the sheriff took his time getting out of the car.

"Did he lose his handcuffs?" Carrie asked under her breath.

"Be nice. I'll handle this," Shea whispered, reflexively checking her hair in the rearview mirror.

"What seems to be the problem, Officer?" Shea asked when Seth finally came to her window.

"I was looking for you a little while ago, but you weren't home," he replied.

"So I heard," Shea replied. "I can assure you that I didn't leave town, we just went to breakfast."

Seth peered in the Jeep. "Morning, Carrie," he said.

She nodded once in return.

"You came out to my house without calling first?" Shea asked, before Carrie could work up a scathing comment.

Seth stared at her for a moment. "I guess I didn't realize that I needed to check with you first," he said.

"Now hold on just a minute, Seth," Shea said. "If you were coming out for personal reasons, then of course you didn't have to check with me first. But if you were coming out to arrest me for a murder I did not commit, since you've been treating me like a suspect, a phone call first would have been nice."

"Why, so you could pack your bags and get away?" The corner of his mouth twitched upward.

"No, so I could make arrangements for Carrie to have help with the farm," Shea replied, her sense of humor having disappeared with the sight of flashing lights behind her Jeep. "And I'm sorry, I don't find anything remotely funny about that."

"Whoa, tiger. How about you just take a breath and listen to me?" Seth said. "I stopped by to let you know that you've been officially cleared as a person of interest in the case."

"Wait…what?"

"He said you've been cleared…" Carrie began.

"I know what he said," Shea interrupted, grinning at her daughter. Then she turned to frown at Seth. "You really could have led with that you know."

"Yeah, I could have, but it was way more fun to see you sputtering like Clarence on a rainy day," Seth said, grinning. "You were cleared early this morning. I'm sure you've noticed that I've been staying away lately, and I want you to know that's been intentional, not because I didn't want to see you, or because I thought you were guilty, but because I didn't want anyone accusing me of playing favorites in this investigation."

"Aside from you stopping by to tell me about it in the first place," Shea said, raising an eyebrow and almost concealing her amusement. Almost.

"Yeah, aside from that," Seth said, flashing those incredible dimples.

"So…now what?" Shea asked. "Have you guys figured out who did this to her? Has there been an arrest?"

"Hold up now," Seth said, raising his hands in mock surrender. "No one has been arrested just yet. But I have a feeling you might know a little bit about what happened to Chelsea."

"I'm sure I don't know what you mean," Shea said, averting her eyes.

"Uh-huh. Where did you go for breakfast just now?" Seth asked her.

"Are you asking me as the sheriff?" Shea shot back cheekily. "Or as my…whatever."

"As your whatever," Seth said, giving her a look that made her blush.

Carrie cleared her throat as if to remind them of her presence.

"Seriously, Shea. Where were you?"

Shea drummed the steering wheel with her index fingers. "Okay, fine. I was out at Russell's Diner talking to Billy Russell and his mom and dad," she admitted.

"You just showed up there and happened to have a chat with the husband of the woman who was murdered." Seth's brows rose. "How'd you manage that?"

"What do you mean, how did I manage that? I just went there and ordered breakfast and we started talking," Shea replied, avoiding his gaze.

"Hey, Mom, I have a great idea," Carrie interjected. "How about you two take me home and go over all of this on your own?" she suggested.

Shea turned to face her, seeming a bit dazed. "Oh, Carrie, yeah, of course. Sorry, honey. Seth, do you want to follow me home and then we can go grab a bite to eat or something?"

"I thought you just ate." He smiled like the cat who ate the canary.

"I uh…left before I finished my food."

"I see." Seth craned his neck to look over at Carrie. "You mad at me?" he asked.

"Mad doesn't even begin to describe it, *Sheriff*."

"Fair enough." Seth nodded. He tapped the door of the Jeep with his hand. "I'll be right behind you, Shea."

CHAPTER ELEVEN

Shea pulled into the parking lot of the White Bass Marina and Lounge and parked behind Seth's pickup truck. He'd decided that it would be more prudent for him to go home and change into civilian clothes before dining with a former person of interest, so they agreed to meet there.

Carrie hadn't said a word when Shea dropped her off but had gone immediately inside to change into chore clothes.

Shea was touched by how protective her daughter was. The young lady had a mama bear streak in her a mile wide. It would come in handy when she became a parent herself.

Seth stood and came to escort her to their table, one hand in the small of her back as they went.

"How about an appetizer and a glass of sweet tea to start?" he suggested, pulling her chair out for her.

"That sounds great to me. Brisket nachos?" Shea asked, entirely aware of the intoxicating scent of his cologne.

"A girl after my own heart." Seth smiled. "Now, tell me what happened when you were at the diner."

"Not much, actually. They told me that Chelsea's marriage had been over for a while and that there was another man named Beau Price who was involved with her. Bill Sr. seemed like a guy with a short fuse and a long temper."

"We already knew about the boyfriend," Seth replied, nodding. He stopped speaking when the server brought their drinks around. "The Russell family has been questioned at length, beginning with Billy. But we're not any closer to the truth than we were before."

"But, what about Beau Price?" Shea's brows rose.

"Sorry, can't comment on that. Ongoing investigation and all." Seth shrugged. "But we've already questioned him."

"And you're not considering him a suspect?"

"I can't confirm or deny."

"Understood," Shea said, sighing. "But I have to ask. Is talking about what I learned the only reason you wanted to grab lunch together?"

Seth shook his head and laughed.

"What?" Shea said, tapping on her plate with her fork.

"For someone who is so good at digging up information, sometimes you miss what's right under that cute little nose of yours." Seth employed the dimples with expert precision.

"You know, I've noticed something about you, Sheriff Seth Grayson."

"And what might that be, Ms. Shea Beaumont?"

"Whenever you want to avoid answering a question, you detonate the one weapon that always succeeds in making me blush."

"I like it when you blush, but I have no idea what you mean by detonating a weapon. I'm pretty sure I have no such weapon."

"You do."

"Oh yeah, and what might that be?"

"Those unfair and entirely effective dimples of yours."

"Huh?" Seth seemed genuinely surprised.

"Don't act like you don't know."

"I don't. I have dimples?" he asked.

"Yes. Yes, you do. And they're an absolutely unfair advantage."

This time when Seth Grayson smiled, he blushed harder than Shea. "I'm sure I don't know what you mean."

"Play your cards right and maybe you'll find out."

After their impromptu date, Shea slowed down to pull into her driveway and was surprised to see Helen

Porter across the street in her farm stand. She pulled over and stopped.

"I didn't know you'd be here today, Helen," she said.

"I was surprised when you and Trish weren't out here today," Helen replied. "Where were you?"

"Well, I went out for breakfast and then met the sheriff for lunch," Shea replied, willing herself not to blush.

"You were out trying to solve that girl's murder, weren't you," Helen said, studying her.

Shea gasped in surprise. "What? I…I'm shocked that you'd say something like that, Helen," she sputtered.

Helen shook her head and smiled. "No, you're just surprised that I figured out what you were doing," she said.

"Okay," Shea said, chuckling and trying to recover. "How in the world did you even think to ask me that?"

"It's not like it takes a rocket scientist to figure you out, girl," Helen replied. "It wasn't that long ago that you and Trish were on the case when my husband was murdered. I saw you in action then, and this time you have even more of an incentive." She shrugged.

"Proving my own innocence is pretty motivating," Shea agreed.

"Are you going to tell me what you found out?" Helen asked, hands on her hips.

"There isn't much to tell," Shea replied. She wasn't about to spill her guts to the town gossip.

"There must be something to tell," Helen said slyly. "Do you want to know how else I figured out what you were doing today?"

"Sure, Helen, why not?" Shea said.

Helen smiled like the Cheshire cat. "You and Trish are both pretty obsessive about being here day in and day out. But the one time that I decided to show up on non-official farmer's market day, the two of you were nowhere to be seen."

"That's fair." Shea nodded.

"I may be old, but I'm not dumb," Helen said. "I also realized that Trish might be worried about being available in case her best friend needed her."

"Maybe you're the one who should be out investigating, Helen," Shea teased. "The good news is that when I met with the sheriff for lunch, he informed me that I am no longer considered a person of interest in the case."

Helen frowned. "He told you that? What does that mean?" she asked. "Is a person of interest the same thing as a suspect?"

"Suspect is a stronger word, but it's basically the same thing," Shea said, not knowing enough about the intricacies of the law to be able to explain it adequately.

"But does he know about the fight the two of you had here on Saturday? I mean, surely you're the only person who would have had a reason to kill her," she said. "Everyone else in this town loved her."

Shea tilted her head to the side and peered closely at the older woman. "Helen, if I didn't know better, I'd think that you wanted me to be charged with Chelsea Russell's murder," she said. "Are you disappointed that I was removed from the persons of interest list?"

Helen blanched, and she swallowed hard. "Oh no, of course not," she insisted. "Not at all. I've just been trying to puzzle things out from all the different angles, you know. I just hear things here and there and try to fit them together, that's all. It's sort of like watching an old episode of 'Murder, She Wrote.' But then, that's probably before your time."

"I know the series," Shea said. "But I can tell you that investigating a crime is no fun when your name is on the list of possible suspects."

"Well, I'm going to pack up. Not many customers today anyway. See you next week," Helen said, pulling down the latch that caused the awnings over her stand to slam down tight.

"Not if I see you first," Shea muttered.

"What's that?" Helen called out from behind the closed-up stand.

"I said have a good day."

CHAPTER TWELVE

Shea drove up the drive toward home and parked out front.

"Hey, Mom," Carrie greeted her from the couch when she walked in.

"Hey CareBear. Want to come help me with the chores? I just need to get changed first."

"They're already done, no worries."

"Oh, you are truly the best. You busy?" Shea asked.

"I'll be free in a few. I'm doing an article on effective fertilization techniques for root vegetables. Why, did you need something?"

"Nope, not at all. I'm going to go admire your handiwork for a bit and maybe we can hang out or something after I get back in."

"Going to go change and run your fingers through the dirt again?" Carrie teased.

"Yeah, I am." Shea chuckled.

"Cool. I'll put on some water for tea when I hear the barn door shut," Carrie offered.

"You're the best. Do you think you might want to adopt me?"

"Nah, you're way too much trouble." Carrie laughed and went back to typing.

Shea changed quickly and headed for the kitchen door, Samson at her heels.

"Don't think I don't know that you just pretend to like me so that you'll get a treat." She laughed, ruffling the hair at the back of his neck as he accompanied her to the fields.

Once Shea knelt down to examine her newly planted tomatoes, Samson tore off, chasing butterflies and living his best doggie life. When Shea headed for the greenhouse to pick some salad veggies, he continued sniffing and playing and enjoying the cool weather and late afternoon sunshine.

With a basketful of fresh goodies, Shea looked around for Samson and saw him near the goat pen, nose to nose with one of the new kids.

"He's making friends." Shea chuckled. "Hey, Sammie boy! You coming inside?" she called out. The only indication that he'd heard her was the waving of his plume of a tail, but he stayed where he was, doing a play bow in front of the kid before darting away toward the barn.

"Silly dog." Shea laughed, heading for the house.

Samson often stayed outside until the sun began to slip from the sky, and he never wandered far.

Shea washed the fresh veggies in the sink and started chopping up cucumbers, carrots, tomatoes, lettuce, and spinach for salad. Carrie wandered out into the kitchen and sat at the table with her, keeping her company.

Suddenly, Carrie sat up straight in her chair, cocking her head to the side. "Mom, do you hear that?" she asked, looking alarmed.

"What?" Shea asked, stopping in mid-chop.

A low keening sound reached their ears. A dog whimpering.

"Samson!" they said in unison, both of them bolting for the door.

The dog was limping toward them from the garden, moving slowly toward the house, but he sat down hard on his rump and slowly slipped onto his side when he reached the driveway. Shea reached him first and he weakly thumped his tail.

"What happened, buddy," she asked, examining him from head to toe. He was panting as though he'd just run a mile, and when Shea looked into his face, she saw that it was swollen on one side.

"Carrie, go get my keys and purse and open the back of the Jeep – we've got to get him to the vet," she ordered, her heart gripped with fear.

She gently hoisted all seventy pounds of Samson up and carried him to the Jeep, where Carrie had already arranged a blanket for him. Shea set him down carefully and raced to the driver's seat.

"I'll stay back here with him," Carrie said, her voice steady, despite the fear in her eyes.

"Try to keep him still. I'll get there as fast as I can."

"Hang in there, buddy," Shea whispered as she sped toward the vet clinic. She dialed the number of the vet clinic and sent the call through the Jeep's speakers so that her hands would be free to drive.

"Dr. Bev's office," a chirpy voice answered.

"Something is wrong with my dog," Shea said, her words tumbling out quickly.

"What's the dog's name?"

"Samson."

"Last name? We have a number of dogs named Samson in our system."

"Beaumont," Shea said quickly. "My name is Shea, his name is Samson. I don't know what's wrong with him, but he's not doing well."

"I understand, that can be scary, but you need to calm down and tell me his symptoms," the receptionist replied.

"Right. Okay, he came limping out of the garden and collapsed on the driveway," Shea said, trying to speak more slowly. "He seems like he's having trouble breathing and his face is swollen."

"Okay, sounds like you probably need to bring him in, then."

"I'm on my way in right now," Shea said. "I should be there in ten minutes."

"Well, I'll need to check the book to see if we have an opening for him."

"You need to make time for him," Shea insisted, her voice raising to a level usually reserved for correcting Clarence when he was about to attack.

"Ma'am, I know that you're upset, but if you don't calm down, I'm going to have to hang up on you," the receptionist replied.

Shea glanced in her rearview mirror. Carrie's expression was grave and Samson's face had become even more swollen since they'd been on the road. She turned her attention back to the woman on the other end of the phone and inhaled deeply to try to dial back her temper a bit. But before she could speak, she heard muffled voices on the other end of the phone. A second later, Dr. Bev came on the line.

"How far out are you, Shea?" she asked.

"Less than ten minutes," Shea replied, nearly wilting with relief. "His face is swelling bigger."

"Can you hear him panting," Dr Bev asked.

"Yes. He's in the back of the Jeep with Carrie, but I can hear him clear up here. It sounds more like he's snoring," Shea said.

"Okay, stay on the phone with me. How far are you from town?"

"About a mile from town," Shea said. "Why? What's wrong with him?" she asked, her stomach in knots, a river of tears barely held at bay.

"Where was he when you found him?"

"He was coming out of the garden when we heard him whimpering," Shea told her. "He made it to the driveway and collapsed."

"Did you see a wound or any blood," Dr. Bev asked.

Shea glanced in the rearview mirror and saw Carrie nod. "Yeah, he has blood on his chest, Mom. There isn't much, but it's there."

"What could be wrong with him?" Shea asked.

"Are you in the parking lot yet?" Dr. Bev ignored her question.

"I just pulled in," Shea told her.

"Park as close to the door as you can," Dr. Bev instructed. "We'll come out and get him. Just open the back of the Jeep and stay out of the way."

Shea pulled up in front of the door, threw the shift into park, and jumped out. She raced to the back, where Carrie had already opened the door and waited. Samson's head was in Carrie's lap, and he thumped his tail lightly just once when he saw Shea and stayed focused on her as she stroked one of his velvety ears.

Seconds later, Dr. Bev and two members of her staff pushed a small gurney over to the Jeep and gently removed a still-conscious Samson, carefully placing him on the gurney. Bev carefully raised his head and looked into his eyes with a flashlight as they rushed him inside. Shea followed the gurney through the lobby and into the back of the clinic while Carrie parked the Jeep in the lot and came charging in afterward.

"What's wrong with him?" Shea asked, Carrie's arm going around her waist as the two of them hovered near the table in the treatment room.

Dr. Beverly gave her staff several orders and placed an intravenous line after quickly shaving Samson's paw, near his ankle. Another tech clad in blue scrubs came in carrying two vials of medicine. Dr. Bev picked up the vials and examined the labels.

"This isn't the correct medication," she told the tech brusquely. "Where's Corky? Tell her I need her in here right now - go!"

Shea and Carrie huddled miserably together, watching silently from the back of the room while Dr. Bev barked out orders and instructions. In less than a minute, Corky sprinted from the room and was back in a flash with another set of vials.

"Okay. Those are the correct meds," Dr. Bev said, filling a syringe with the first medication and sending it through the I.V. She followed it with the second medication, then examined the small wound on his chest. "He is breathing better now," she announced, seconds later.

"Oh, thank goodness," Shea said shakily as the room swam around her.

"How about you sit for a minute?" Carrie suggested, leading her to a chair.

Shea sat down and took a deep breath. Dr. Bev pulled a stool up next to her and patted her on the knee.

"Okay, while Dan cleans up his wound let me tell you what's going on," she said, as Carrie stood behind her mother's chair, hands on her shoulders. "It appears that Samson here had a fight with a snake and he lost. Based on his reaction to the bite, I think he was bitten by a venomous snake."

"A venomous snake?" A wave of nausea rolled through Shea and Carrie's hands tightened a bit on her shoulders.

"It was probably a copperhead and not a rattlesnake. Despite the reaction, I think he is going to be okay," Dr. Bev said. "I also think he had a little bit more serious of a reaction to the bite because this probably isn't his first rodeo with a copperhead. He wasn't in complete anaphylactic shock, but his reaction tells me he has been bitten before."

"Wait, if you're not sure whether it was a rattler or a copperhead, how do you know which medicine you needed to use?" Shea asked, alarmed. "What if you got the wrong one?"

"It's okay, Mom. They're both pit vipers, so she would have used the same meds, right Dr. Bev?" Carrie asked.

"Very good." Dr. Bev nodded her approval.

"Is he going to make it?" Shea asked, reaching for Carrie's hand.

Dr. Bev smiled and nodded. "We're going to keep him here for a couple of days just to make sure he gets some IV pain meds and stays hydrated, but yes, he's going to make it. You did a great job of getting him here in time. Why don't you two head out and we'll get him set up for the evening. You can come back and visit him first thing in the morning, and I'll let you know if anything changes overnight. I know he gave you a scare, but take my word for it, Samson is not the first curious pup to go one on one with a snake."

"Thank you," Shea breathed, standing so slowly. Before leaving the room, she and Carrie both went over to a now sleeping Samson, who was breathing just fine.

"Get better, my sweet boy," Shea whispered, kissing the top of his head. "We'll be back tomorrow." Carrie said her goodbyes as well and the two of them headed for the door.

Shea hesitated once they were outside the treatment room, not sure where to go next. She'd never been back to the emergency area of the clinic.

They headed down a hallway that she believed would lead them to the lobby and could hear voices on the other side of a door as she passed.

"Messed up the medication again," a woman's voice said. "What is going on around here?"

"I don't get it. Doctor Beverly went over everything in the lab a week ago. I just don't understand," a man's voice said.

"Seems like Corky is the only one who knows where everything goes, though," the woman said.

"You better be careful," Corky said, startling Shea and Carrie. Her face was twisted into a frown. "Eavesdropping is a very bad habit."

"Oh, thank goodness you're here. We're not eavesdropping, we're lost. I've never been back to the emergency area and Dr. Bev gave us directions to get out, but we got all turned around somehow. Stress, I guess. Can you point us toward the lobby?"

Corky's smile returned. "Sure, no problem. We've had people throw up in the hallways because of stress, so you guys are doing fine. Just head right out that way." She pointed. "…and follow the arrows to the front."

"Oh, wow, I didn't even see the arrows." Shea shook her head.

"No worries. They don't even start until you get past the lab," Corky said.

Shea thanked her again and they headed for the lobby. She left her credit card information with the receptionist and drank in huge gulps of fresh air when they stepped out into the parking lot.

CHAPTER THIRTEEN

"I'm driving," Carrie said firmly, as they headed to the Jeep.

"I'll be okay. It's just...Samson, and being where Chelsea was...it's just a lot," Shea murmured, wondering if she was going to pass out or be sick.

"You're right. It IS a lot, and we don't need to add having a car wreck into the mix. You're as pale as a ghost, Mom. I'm driving," Carrie replied gently.

"I'm so glad you're here, honey," Shea said, bursting into tears. "You don't even know how glad."

Carrie wrapped her mother in a hug, right there in the parking lot. "I'm glad I could be here for you, Mom.

You were always there for me, now it's my turn," she soothed, her breath stirring Shea's hair.

Shea felt safe and warm in her daughter's embrace and took several deep breaths to pull herself together. "Sorry. You know I'm not like this." She chuckled sadly, wiping her face with the back of her sleeve.

"Emotions are healthy, Mom. Come on, let's get you home. There's food in the pantry and beer in the fridge," Carrie joked, putting an arm around Shea's waist to guide her to the passenger side.

"First there are chores to be done," Shea replied, smiling wanly.

"Aaaaand she's back, ladies and gentlemen," Carrie teased.

"We have to get ready for tomorrow's market and we have to be extra careful in the garden. I swear…if I see that snake…"

"We should both take the snake hook and a nice sharp hoe with us, just in case," Carrie suggested. "We want to relocate him if we can, but if we can't, and we're in a bad situation…"

"Good idea," Shea agreed, swinging herself up into the passenger seat. "We should take flashlights too, for the walk back to the house when we're done." She was feeling better now that she had something to focus on, aside from murder and the near death of her beloved companion.

Carrie started the Jeep and pulled out of the parking lot, a pensive look on her face. "Yeah, speaking of the snake…I was thinking…"

"What?" Shea asked, noting the serious tone.

"I mean, I'm not from here, but it seems to me that it's a bit early in the year and a little on the cool side for snakes to be out and about, isn't it?"

Shea thought for a moment. "Yeah, it does seem a little early, but Samson was out chasing butterflies in the sunshine, so if he happened to encounter a nasty critter that was out sunning itself, it would have had the energy and metabolism to strike, I would think."

"That makes sense." Carrie nodded, seeming to get back to concentrating on her driving.

They rode in silence for a while as Shea mulled over the past few days in her mind.

"Well, we're home," Carrie said softly as they both looked at the empty dog bed on the porch. "Do you want me to do the chores? I can work on…" she began.

"Not a chance. We're going out there together. Not just because it's dangerous, but because I really need something to do or I'm just going to be a weepy mess," Shea interrupted.

"Good, we'll get them done twice as fast," Carrie replied with a smile. "Let's get to it."

Determined to not let one vicious predator scare them away, Shea and Carrie took the proper precautions and knocked out the evening chores in record time. The goats and the chickens were all healthy and not stressed, so Shea was satisfied that they hadn't had any reptilian visitors.

When she left the chicken coop, she saw Carrie kneeling down, stroking Clarence's back and speaking to him in low tones.

"Well, I'll be darned," she marveled, moving closer to hear what her daughter was saying.

"Now, Clarence," Carrie said, as the formerly feisty bird stretched his neck so that she could rub the back of it. "We might have a little snake problem around here, so I'm counting on you to let us know if there's any trouble, okay? I know I usually want you to be quiet, but if you see a snake, you start yelling. I promise I won't scold you."

Carrie held her arms out and Shea's jaw dropped open when Clarence hopped into them for a snuggle. "That's a good boy," Carrie cooed as the rooster leaned against her chest.

"If you had told me about this moment, I never would have believed it," Shea said, shaking her head.

Clarence raised his wings and got a familiar look in his eye.

"Be nice," Carrie warned, setting him down. He looked up at her, relaxed his wings, shot Shea a dirty look, and headed back into the chicken coop.

Shea laughed. "I knew you were good with animals, but wow, I had no idea you were a miracle worker."

"He just wants to be loved, too." Carrie smiled and shrugged.

"Unbelievable. Well done, Dr. Doolittle."

"Hey, I don't do little, I do a lot." Carrie chuckled.

"Yes you do, and I'm grateful," Shea replied. "We have a huge harvest to sell tomorrow, and the microgreen people are coming by for an order too, so it's going to be busy. Let's head in."

"Absolutely. I'm starving."

"Me too," Shea agreed. She turned to call for Samson, then remembered and stood still, taking a deep breath.

"Yeah, I miss him too," Carrie said softly, moving to her side. "It was weird doing chores without him. But he'll be back soon."

"Not soon enough," Shea said, swallowing past the lump in her throat. "I think you might need to teach him a command for staying with us during the summer season when he's outside."

"I'm on it," Carrie nodded. "Now, let's go get some dinner."

The two of them finished making the salad that Shea had started prior to Samson's emergency, then supplemented it with country ham and Swiss sandwiches made on Trish's mouthwateringly delicious rye bread, with a smear of spicy mustard.

"Let's take our plates into the living room," Shea suggested. "I just want to be in my comfy chair, with some nonsense show on the TV in the background."

"Sounds perfect," Carrie agreed. "You grab the plates and I'll pour us some iced tea."

"Decaf," Shea replied. "It's late."

"I know." Carrie grinned and shook her head.

Shea took a bite from her sandwich, and as she chewed, she just couldn't shake the thought that she'd forgotten something or was missing something, but she couldn't quite put her finger on it.

"Oh, well." She shrugged. She had a delicious meal in front of her and her daughter's company, so for the moment, she was going to focus on enjoying both. Whatever was bugging her would either go away, or she'd remember what it was.

When she'd beaten back her hunger a bit, Shea's instinct that she had forgotten something returned, frustrating her to no end. She rose to take the now empty dishes and glasses back to the kitchen. "I think I'm going to go in my office and get on the laptop for a bit," she told Carrie.

"Checking on the Russell family's alibi?" Carrie asked, pointing the remote at the TV to turn it off.

"What are you psychic now?" Shea asked.

"Nah, I was just surprised you had the willpower to wait this long."

"Wanna join me?" Shea asked.

"Maybe in a bit. I'm going to start another article for Agriculture Focus."

Shea stared at her daughter, impressed. "What's this one about, pit vipers?"

"Now who's psychic?" Carrie smiled. "Yep, I'm working on the physiological implications of repeated bites from pit vipers. Dr. Bev's analysis made me think, so I'm researching it."

"Wow." Shea blinked. "Are they paying you for these articles?"

"Of course. I figured I'll have my student loans paid off in two years or less if I continue producing at this rate."

Shea grinned. "That's my girl!"

After stashing the dishes in the dishwasher and wiping down the counters, Shea settled in with her laptop, her wonderfully worn leather executive chair welcoming her in its embrace.

She went first to the website of the oil company that employed Bill Sr. and Billy, and from there, she found the company's social media pages. When she cruised through photos of recent events, she found the retirement party, where images of Bill, Sylvia, and Billy were as easy to find as the empty champagne glasses.

Clearly the Russell family had been where they claimed they were on the night of Chelsea's death, so Shea began her next search for Beau Price.

She found a social media profile for him, but it had very little public information on it. He obviously had put his settings on Private mode. From what little Shea could see, there were no photos of Beau and Chelsea together. In fact, the few photos that were visible were of a man considerably older than Billy.

"Sugar daddy?" she mused, ashamed of herself as soon as the words left her lips.

Shea searched for a place of employment and came up with nothing. She searched for photos of Beau with friends. Again, nothing. Frustrated, she closed her computer, determined to take up the search again in the morning, after she hopefully got some sleep.

CHAPTER FOURTEEN

By six a.m., Shea and Carrie were already down at the farm stand, stocked up and ready to greet customers. The owners of the upscale restaurant in Tulsa that had an exclusive contract for microgreens with Shea were due to stop by at seven for their weekly pickup. Coffee in hand, they spotted cars heading their way in the distance and shared a smile. This was why they were here, and it looked like business was going to be good.

A steady flow of customers kept them busy until just before eleven. Shea handed over the last cartons of the early peas to a lucky customer while Carrie began to pack up for the day. Helen Porter arrived just after they started closing things down.

"Are you leaving already?" Helen asked, in the judgmental tone that made Shea's jaws ache.

"Yep, we're sold out and I have to go to the vet's office to check on Samson," Shea replied. "He was bitten by a snake last night and had a pretty severe reaction to the venom."

"Oh, no!" Helen's eyes went wide, and her tone immediately softened. "Is he alright?"

Shea nodded. "Dr. Bev said she thought he would be fine, but she wanted to keep him for a few days to make sure. So, we're going to visit him when we're done here."

"Oh, I hope he is okay. Those darn snakes can sneak right up on you when you least expect it," Helen replied. "Anyway, I just came by to clean out my stand and get ready for a very busy spring. Last time I was here I noticed things needed a little bit of sprucing up."

"Would you like something to eat? I've been handing out samples of a new caprese salad that I made last night, and I have some left," Shea offered.

"Oh, yes, I could definitely eat some of that," Helen replied, waiting while Shea ladled the rest of the salad into a disposable cup and handed it to her with a plastic spoon.

"Oh, this is really good," Helen said when she tried the first bite.

"I'm glad you like it," Shea said. "It got great reviews from customers all morning."

"You better plant more of these herbs and little bitty tomatoes, people are going to want to make this," Helen said, pointing her spoon at Shea. She took another large bite. "By the way, how goes the investigation? Have you found the killer yet?" she asked, casually pushing bits of tomato and herb around with her spoon.

Shea shook her head. "Nope, not even close. I'm going to talk to Chelsea's boyfriend, Beau Price, if I can find out where he is."

"Price?" Helen thought for a moment. "I think he lives north of town. His parents have a big farm up that way," she said. "In fact, I think Beau is their middle son."

"North of town?" Shea confirmed.

Helen nodded. "Yep, I'm pretty sure. His folks have several hundred acres. They run cattle," she said. "I think the sons work the farm for their parents now."

"Good to know, thanks," Shea said.

"You're quite welcome. Thanks for the salad, Shea," Helen said, tossing her empty cup and spoon into the trash barrel next to the stand. "And don't forget to keep an eye out, you gotta be real careful about those snakes in the grass. You never know where you're going to come across one."

Shea nodded absently and went back to helping Carrie load their empty wooden vegetable crates into the back of the wagon. After they'd finished, she drove the tractor with its attached load up to the barn, where they unloaded the wagon and parked the tractor.

Refreshed after a quick shower, Shea finally felt ready to make another attempt to figure things out. She dressed quickly, checked her reflection in the mirror, then headed back downstairs where Carrie was already dressed and ready. On her way to town, she called Trish and asked her about the Price farming family.

"They live about two miles north of town on Farm Road twenty-four," Trish told her. "Are you going up there to talk to them about the farmer's market?" Trish's tone was instructive.

Shea glanced over at Carrie smiled. "Why yes, that's exactly why we're headed up there," she said.

"What a great idea," Trish said. "Since we're always looking for new vendors. But Shea, don't get too pushy. If Beau Price is the one who…hurt Chelsea, you need to watch yourself around him. Text me when you get there. If I don't hear from you fifteen minutes later, I am sending in the cavalry."

"Got it," Shea said. "Thank you, my friend." She hung up and headed for the highway north.

"Umm…Mom…aren't we supposed to be going to the vet clinic?" Carrie asked.

"We'll get over there after this. I have a hunch, Care-Bear and I think we need to follow it. Dr. Bev would have called us if Samson wasn't doing well, and this shouldn't take long," Shea explained.

She found the farm road in short order and slowed her Jeep when she spotted a large metal machine shed. There were several driveways leading into and out of the farm and before she could choose one to pull into, a flat-bed pickup with a large hay spike on the back pulled out and slowed down next to her.

"Can I help you, ma'am?" the driver asked. Shea studied his face. He resembled the few photos of Beau Price she had seen on the internet, and her stomach did a little flip flop.

"I hope so, I'm looking for a member of the Price family," Shea replied with a smile.

"And why would you want to speak with a member of the Price family?" he asked. His hair was cut close to his head, sandy brown sprinkled with gray, at least what she could see beneath the band of his ball cap. She took note of his light blue eyes.

"Because I run the farmer's market west of town, just north of the lake," Shea said. "I wanted to reach out and let you know that we have space for more vendors. I am reaching out to some of the bigger farmers in the area."

"You're talking about the old Bartholomew place, right?"

Shea nodded. "I bought it almost two years ago," she said. "I wasn't sure if your farm grew vegetables or not."

"Well, no," the man pushed his hat back further on his head. "Not really. Right now it's just me and my youngest brother, Bobby."

"Are you the owner of the farm?"

"No, ma'am," he said with a grin. "That'd be my daddy. I'm Mike and my brothers Beau and Bobby and me run this place usually. But lately it's just been me and Bobby."

"Where is Beau?" Shea asked too quickly. She winced inwardly, then tried to recover. "That's the name of your other brother, right?"

Mike Price nodded. "He's up in Wisconsin, looking for more land of his own."

"How long has he been gone?" Shea asked.

"Over a month," Mike said with a shrug. He cocked his head to the side. "Why are you so curious about my brother? You aren't asking around because of the death of that girl, are you? Because if you are, you can just see yourself out of here."

"Mom, I think we should go see Samson now," Carrie said. Shea ignored her.

"No, I'm really here about the farmer's market," Shea said. "But I have to admit, I am a little curious about Beau and what happened. The sheriff's department hauled me in first thing to ask me about an interaction I had with Chelsea. I know I didn't kill her. I barely knew her." Shea shrugged.

"And you heard that Beau had taken up with her and it's always the boyfriend, ain't it?" Mike snapped, the dancing light gone from his blue eyes. "Well, I got news for you, lady. Beau cut things off with her more than two months ago. And before you ask me why, it's because she won't listen to a thing he tells her. He tried to tell her to be careful, but she wouldn't listen to him and now look at what happened."

"I'm sorry, I wasn't trying to be disrespectful. I'll be on my way, but I just have a quick question - why would Beau have to tell her to be careful? Was she in danger?"

"I'd think that's kind of obvious at this point," Mike said, raising an eyebrow. "She had a bad habit of turning a blind eye to the things going on around her, especially at work. Some of those folks she works with are bad news. I mean, really bad news. A couple of the women in that place are hitched to some of the worst men in this whole dang county. Max Sims is right there at the top of the dung heap."

"Max Sims? As in, Corky Sims?"

"You got it, lady. Beau tried to tell Chelsea about that whole family, but she wouldn't listen," Mike shook his head, pulled down on the gear shift and began to back up.

"Wait," Shea shouted to be heard above the engine roar. "What's so bad about the Sims family?"

Mike Price hit the brakes and stared at her. "I forget you ain't from around here," he said. "Max Sims comes from a long line of drug dealers. I can't even believe his old lady got a job anywhere near a place that stocks medicines. It's kind of like putting an arsonist's wife to work in a fireworks factory." With that, he put the flatbed pickup into reverse and turned around in the driveway. Shea drove further up the road and pulled up in the last driveway, to turn around and head back to town.

"Well, that was quite the revelation," Carrie said. "I normally wouldn't say this, but could you please speed a little bit?"

"You're darn right I will. We need to see a vet about a snake in the grass."

Dr. Bev was in her office when Shea waved at the receptionist in the lobby and breezed past. She didn't wait for an invitation to head back and check on Samson.

"Oh, Shea," the vet called out when she and Carrie powerwalked past the office doorway. "Hang on, I can take you back to check on Samson." She hurried to fall in beside the determined mother and daughter duo. "He had a pretty good night. I did have to give him another dose of antihistamine around two this morning."

"Were you here with him all night?" Shea asked.

"Yes," Dr. Bev replied. "I tend to do that when I have a serious patient. Plus, he's awfully cute." She smiled.

"He definitely is," Shea agreed. "I have a question for you, and it might be a little…awkward."

"I practice medicine, nothing shocks me." Dr. Bev chuckled. "Ask away."

"Yesterday, when I brought Samson in, there seemed to be some problem with the medication that was brought to you, and right after that, when I headed back out to the lobby, I got a little lost and I overheard a couple of your workers discussing the issue."

"What are you getting at, Shea?" Dr. Bev stopped in her tracks and folded her arms.

"Look, I know your office has been through a lot recently," Shea said. "But I can't help but wonder if there are some really awful things going on around here. Things that have been kept from you."

"I'm not sure I'm following what you're saying," the vet said. "What could you possibly think is going on around here?"

"I just know that one plus one equals two most of the time," Shea said. "I see a very busy clinic and an unexplained murder. I also see and hear that there is an issue with pharmaceuticals. It's not much of a stretch to think that there just might be something connecting those things."

"Shea, that's a very serious…" Dr. Bev began, only to be interrupted by shouts from the other side of the clinic. After a quick apology to Shea, she took off running. Shea and Carrie weren't more than two strides behind her.

Dr. Beverly ran toward the back of the building and pushed through the double doors where the kennels for the animals who were inpatients were kept. It sounded like every dog in the place was barking like their lives depended on it. Several vet techs were gathered in a semicircle, all shouting at once. Shea noticed the tech named Dan and the two techs she had overheard in the hallway were there.

Corky Sims was on the floor next to Samson, who was out of his kennel, his collar firmly in her grasp. She held a syringe aloft in her other hand.

Shea made a move to charge forward, but Carrie held her in an iron grip. "Don't, Mom. Samson might get hurt." She choked back a sob.

"Don't you do it, Corky," Dan thundered. "Don't you hurt that dog!"

"What on earth is going on here?" Dr. Bev demanded. "Corky, let go of the dog immediately."

"We caught her, Doctor Bev," another vet tech said.

"Caught her doing what, Alexis," Dr. Bev asked her. "What's in that syringe?"

"Ketamine," Dan answered for her. "I think we've finally gotten to the bottom of the problem in the pharmacy."

"You need to watch your mouth or I'm going to administer this medication," Corky threatened from the floor.

Samson whined and gazed up at Shea, his eyes pleading.

"I swear in the name of all that is holy…" Shea began, biting off her words when Carrie squeezed her hand and whispered, "Stop."

"Someone had better start talking," Dr. Bev said.

"Dan caught Corky in the lab with fourteen vials of Ketamine," Alexis said. "She also had a copy of the medication log with her."

Dr. Bev knelt down about five feet from Corky. "Is this true, Corky? Have you been stealing drugs from the clinic?"

"You'd better get out of my way," Corky growled. "I'm going to stand up and walk right out of here and heaven help you if any of you get in my way."

"Let her go," Dr. Bev said, standing up and backing away. "If she's guilty of stealing drugs the sheriff will catch up with her. Alright, Corky, you just let go of Samson and you can walk right out the door."

"Nice try, but that's not happening," Corky said.

"Hey!" Carrie shouted suddenly, staring at Corky, distracting her while Shea lunged, barreling into the maniacal vet tech.

Before Corky knew it, Shea knocked her flat on her back and slammed down the hand holding the syringe, making her drop it. Shea sat on Corky's stomach, her knees pinning the out-of-control tech's hands to the floor. With one hand she gripped Corky's jaw and looked her right in the eye.

"You listen to me you smug little brat. After what you were about to do to my dog, you should be grateful that I'm going to let the sheriff handle this. I'm sure that your fellow prisoners in the county jail will be much kinder to you than I would be."

Shea was staring so intently at Corky, daring her to try something, that she didn't realize at first that a large, strong hand was shaking her shoulder.

"Shea?" she heard Seth say, though he sounded miles away. "I've got this, okay. Just ease up, now. The syringe is secured. Samson is safe with Carrie. Come on now," he said gently.

Dan secured Corky's hands so that Shea could stand up without being attacked, and Dr. Bev helped her to her feet while Seth read Corky her rights and handcuffed her.

"She was here, Bev. She was here that night that Chelsea was killed. It had to be her. I don't know why, but it had to be," Shea murmured, dazed.

"I know, Shea. Alexis checked a missing video footage tape that she found in Corky's car. But let's not worry about that right now, okay? Right now, you're in shock and I'm going to take good care of you."

CHAPTER FIFTEEN

"I still don't get how you figured it all out," Trish said the next day. They were seated on the edge of the flatbed. It was the first midweek farmer's market of the spring, and the crowds had been less than enthusiastic. "How did you manage to eliminate all of the men in Chelsea's life as suspects and figure out that it was her coworker?"

"It was actually Helen that made something click for me," Shea said. "She started talking about snakes in the grass and how you have to watch out for them. As soon as I figured out that Beau Price wasn't even in the picture, I knew."

"But what gave her away? Was it what Mike Price had to say about the Sims family?"

Shea nodded. "That more or less confirmed my suspicions, yeah," she said. "You should have seen the look on Corky's face when she caught me listening in on her coworkers. She wasn't just disapproving because I was eavesdropping, she was furious. Her face even twisted up in a weird way. I figured that someone who could get that angry, that quickly, probably not only had something to hide, but might just be capable of murder." Shea shuddered.

"Right before I drove out to the Price farm, I had the weirdest feeling that I was forgetting something, and when Mike Price said what he did about Max Sims and his wife, it all fell into place. I remembered that awful face she made, and then I remembered what Helen had said about snakes in the grass.

"It's still hard to believe that such a tiny person could squeeze the life out of someone else," Trish said.

"Yeah, but you'd be surprised what desperation can do for your strength," Shea said, chuckling.

"Right? I heard what you did at the clinic, Wonder Woman. Girl, I would have paid good money to see you straight up tackle that evil woman." Trish chuckled.

"I'm just glad Carrie had the presence of mind to distract her when she saw me start to move, otherwise I might have been pumped full of a lethal dose of Ketamine."

"Then I'd have gone to jail for taking out the murderer of my best friend. It would've been a whole mess," Trish mused. "Well now, speaking of incarceration, here comes trouble," she nodded toward the road.

Shea's heart leapt when she recognized Seth's pickup turning into her drive.

"Dang, sweetie, you're blushing before he even gets out of the truck now?" Trish teased. "I guess I'd better leave the two of you alone. I'll be in my stand when he leaves, so you can fill me in on everything."

"Trish," Seth nodded to her as she passed by on her way out of Shea's stand.

"Sheriff," Trish smirked, turning back to wink at Shea, who blushed even harder.

"I have good news, Shea, so I thought I'd come on out and tell you myself," Seth announced, accepting the cup of coffee that Carrie handed him.

"Do tell," Shea said, trying to stop grinning from ear to ear.

"I just ran into Dr. Bev, and she said that Samson is ready to come home."

"Oh, thank goodness," Carrie breathed.

"What a relief, it's been so weird around here without that furry guy," Shea replied.

"Well, go get him, Mom! I can handle the stand," Carrie practically shoved Shea out of the door.

"I'm so excited I don't even know if I can drive," Shea said, laughing with delight.

"Well, get in the truck then, I'll drive." Seth shrugged.

"Really? You don't mind him being in the back of your pickup?"

"Are you serious? It's Samson. That boy is gonna ride home right up front with us. If I'm going to be hanging around here a bunch, we might as well get him used to the truck," Seth replied.

"Are you going to be around here a bunch?" Shea asked, her heart hammering in her chest.

"That's the plan, Shea," Seth said, tipping her chin up and giving her a quick kiss on the tip of her nose. "If that's alright with you, that is."

Shea couldn't speak, but she was quite certain that her eyes were telling him everything he needed to know.

ALSO BY SUMMER PRESCOTT

Check out all the books in Summer Prescott's catalog!

Summer Prescott Book Catalog

AUTHOR'S NOTE

I'd love to hear your thoughts on my books, the storylines, and anything else that you'd like to comment on—reader feedback is very important to me. My contact information, along with some other helpful links, is listed on the next page. If you'd like to be on my list of "folks to contact" with updates, release and sales notifications, etc.… just shoot me an email and let me know. Thanks for reading!

Also…

… if you're looking for more great reads, Summer Prescott Books publishes several popular series by outstanding Cozy Mystery authors.

CONTACT SUMMER PRESCOTT BOOKS PUBLISHING

Twitter: @summerprescott1

Bookbub: https://www.bookbub.com/authors/summer-prescott

Blog and Book Catalog: http://summerprescottbooks.com

Email: summer.prescott.cozies@gmail.com

YouTube: https://www.youtube.com/channel/UCngKNUkDdWuQ5k7-Vkfrp6A

And…be sure to check out the Summer Prescott Cozy Mysteries fan page and Summer Prescott Books Publishing Page on Facebook – let's be friends!

CONTACT SUMMER PRESCOTT BOOKS PUBLISHING

To download a free book, and sign up for our fun and exciting newsletter, which will give you opportunities to win prizes and swag, enter contests, and be the first to know about New Releases, click here: http://summerprescottbooks.com

Printed in Great Britain
by Amazon